Black Bear Lake

Leslie Liautaud

BLUE HANDLE PUBLISHING

Copyright © 2022

LESLIE LIAUTAUD

For information about bulk, educational and other special discounts, please contact Blue Handle Publishing.

To book Leslie Liautaud for any event, contact Blue Handle Publishing: www.bluehandlepublishing.com

Cover & Interior Design: Blue Handle Publishing and Existence Creative/John Kraynak

Editing: Book Puma Editorial Services
BookPumaOnline.com

BOOK PUMA

ISBN: 978-1-955058-03-2

For Spencer, Lucy, and Fred:
You will always be my North Stars.

Prologue

MARCH 2008

M y eyes shot open and darted around, searching for clues in the darkness. I gulped for air. A suffocating panic punched me in the sternum and my heart pounded, a barrel drum reverberating in my ears and my rib cage threatening to crack open with each pump. Sweat pooled in the crevices of my collarbone as salty droplets formed along my upper lip.

I jerked my head toward the faint tick of the second hand on a clock. 3:24 a.m. My breathing slowed as I recognized the room. Our room. I turned to Julie. Her chest rose and fell rhythmically, evidence she was sleeping in complete peace. I watched for a moment and listened to the gentle whoosh of her inhale, the purr of her exhale. A tip of hair fanned out on her pillow, and I fingered the edges gingerly. Touching her was like caressing a talisman. She was everything that represented goodness, strength, and courage. It had been that way from the moment we met.

Sliding out from under the heavy down comforter, I shivered as hot air evaporated from my body. Slowing my movements to avoid waking Julie, I crept to the bathroom window, slid the frame open, and thrust my head out. The sharp March air slapped my face as I filled my lungs, over and over. They burned with a cold, painful pleasure that wrenched me away from my nightmare.

The dream was occurring with more frequency, each time

returning me to the one place I wanted to escape.

In my sleep, I was a teen again.

Dannie was at my side, her hand in mine.

And we were back at Black Bear Lake.

Chapter 1

MAY 2008

E verything hurt.

The pavement too hard on my dragging feet, the wind too cold on my cheeks, the sun too bright for my eyes. My coat too scratchy. My shoes too bulky. Even my head seemed too heavy for my neck, bobbing low, facing the ground as I shuffled down Lincoln Avenue. There was no need to look up. I knew the path well.

Over the last few years, I walked the same route many times, always stopping for a coffee at the local Starbucks. But those monthly visits recently grew to twice a week. Even my wallet was starting to hurt.

At 2418 Lincoln Avenue was an old Chicago brownstone converted into four offices. It sat in the heart of yuppy-ville, power-sprayed clean and surrounded by a stately iron fence. Lincoln Park was a land of golden retrievers and J. Crew models. An area of the city where you worked either in marketing for a trendy PR firm or as a stock analyst for the Chicago Board of Trade. An area where I once belonged. Where I deserved to be. Where I could hide. The brisk wind picked up and people scurried from the street to the sidewalk, holding down their skirts and clasping their trendy camping jackets to their chests. I would've bet my next ten lattes that not one of them had ever stepped foot out of the city, let alone gone camping.

Julie would have laughed at that.

I looked down at my cargo pants. They were a light khaki when I put them on three weeks ago. Since then, they had soured to a dark mustard color. My fisherman's sweater was in no better condition, with food stains on its chest and dark dirt rings around the cuffs.

I punched the security code for the gate, shoving it open and letting it swing freely until it banged closed, watching the fence vibrate, delaying my climb. I closed my eyes and stood on top of the stoop, needing to feel something. I sucked in the freeze and held it. The sharp pain was enough to push my feet through the front entry.

Dr. Marchand's office was on the third floor. I knocked when I reached his landing.

"Come in, Adam."

If not for the diplomas on the wall, you'd swear you were in a designer showroom. The doctor's pricey furniture and original works of art were evidence of his elegant taste and the success of his practice. The office was decorated in neutral tones of beige, taupe, and cream, and I wondered if his choice of a calming palate was more than just good interior design. No exploding greens, shocking blues, or blazing purples. Definitely no fiery reds. Keep the crazy to a minimum.

Dr. Marchand looked up from his corner desk. As usual, his workspace was clean except for one notebook and a pencil. I imagined a secret room in the back housing his *normal person* mess, looking like Dorothy's farmhouse after the tornado. A little yin to his front-office yang.

I shuffled in, sighing as Marchand glanced at me. It was one small flicker of his eye, but I caught it. The miniscule realization that *no progress has been made since I saw you last*.

"Please, sit," the doctor said instead.

I sank into the camel couch. "Morning."

"Good morning."

I stared at his diploma on the wall.

"How are you feeling today?"

I gestured to my unchanged clothes.

Marchand gave a slight nod. "Tell me about the last couple days."

"Same, I guess."

"What's the same?"

"Same as I told you last time."

"Which is what?"

I raised an eyebrow. "I thought you would have marked it down in that notebook of yours. Or weren't you listening?"

The doctor sighed. Some psychologists refuse to show emotion to their patients, afraid it conveys judgment of the patients' feelings, that it will shut them down. Marchand did not fall into that category. Of course, even if he was one of those guys, after seeing me for years, he'd be entitled to show impatience at a smartass statement.

"I listened. But I'm not sure *you* did. I want you to tell me about the last couple of days. I want details. I want you to listen to those details. I want you to hear what's actually going on in your life. I want you to start facing some realities."

Doesn't it show? I thought. *I'm a mess. I'm living my reality.*

"Like what?" I asked.

"Like Julie leaving you."

"What? When did *that* happen?"

"I'm being serious. It's been three weeks and you still haven't told me why she left."

How? How could I tell him that our split wasn't some fissure, some small crack in our foundation? It was an earthquake. The big one that sends California sliding into the ocean.

Marchand sat still for a moment before looking me squarely in the eyes.

"This is why Julie asked you to come here five years ago. To avoid this very scenario."

I knew why she had been concerned. I knew what she wanted me to make peace with. But to do so, I'd have to remember everything. No. That old wound simply couldn't be re-opened. I stared at a small fray in the carpeting.

Marchand continued. "She saw it then. She knew this could be a major issue between you."

My eyes stayed put. "Well, I guess she overestimated me."

"That's just it. If she didn't think you could move past this, she would have left years ago."

"Maybe staying in a dead-end marriage says more about her than about me."

"Is that what you think of Julie? That she's weak?"

"No."

"That she's ignorant?"

My knee began to bounce. "I didn't say that."

"That she deserves to be childless against her will?"

I was trembling all over.

"That after ten years she's the fool?"

She's anything but a fool. My mind drifted.

JULIE WAS SPRAWLED across the bed, one half under the crisp white linen duvet, the other wrapped inside a chenille throw. Her long chestnut hair twisted into a haphazard bun, wearing a threadbare T-shirt of mine.

The Sunday paper was scattered around us as we sipped coffee and pored over the want ads. One of our favorite lazy activities was deciphering the posted descriptions. No one could deceive Julie. Her olive skin crinkled around her eyes as she started to laugh.

"Okay, here's a good one: 1986 Ford Mustang. New paint, new tinted windows, fully refurbished interior."

I paused. "New paint always means some sort of fender bender. New windows definitely mean a crash. Not sure about the interior."

"New interior without a doubt means fire. This guy blew up his car. I wonder what the story is." Giggling, Julie flipped the page with an exaggerated flourish.

That laugh of hers was what captivated me in the first place.

I WAS SUFFERING through an excruciating date, blaming myself for taking out a friend's sister. You can't quit while you're ahead when it's a friend's sister. I sat, nodding politely as she droned about the hardships of selling radio advertising while the radio industry was dying. I fiddled with the edamame on my plate, playing an imaginary soccer game. I shot one through the wasabi goal.

The conversation I was really listening to came from a group of women seated directly behind me. I hadn't turned to look at them, but their easy camaraderie and laughter told me no men were present. Among the chorus of whispers and giggling, one voice hit me in my soft spot. Maybe it was genetic susceptibility, but hearing hers was like listening to a gentle lullaby.

The noise coming from across my table was anything but that.

"...and so, what can I say to the guy? I mean, he wants ten two-minute spots during prime hours of *Marcus in the Morning*. I mean, seriously, like I can give him that?"

"Will you excuse me for one moment?" I rose before she could answer and turned to get a look at the mystery table. I hesitated a half moment and glimpsed at the creature, her head thrown back, tears of laughter pooling in the corners of her eyes. I walked to the bathroom feeling as if I'd gulped a gallon of laughing gas. Cheap pick-up lines ran through my brain, but none fit. She deserved better.

I meandered back to the table, trying to pass the last of my obligatory time with Miss Radiohead. Then, there *she* was, walking toward me. Walking toward the bathroom, really, but heading in my direction. It was a now-or-never moment. I smiled, then froze, my tongue as large as a cantaloupe, blocking the escape of any sound from my mouth.

She stopped in front of me and, with shocking self-confidence, held out her hand.

"Hi, I'm Julie." She smiled.

"Adam," I mumbled as my lips formed an irrepressibly juvenile grin.

"I saw you sitting at a table near mine. Sorry if we're bothering your date."

"No. Not at all. And it's not a date."

Her eyebrows rose skeptically.

"I mean, it's a date, but it's a first date and it's a friend's sister and, you know, it's not really—"

Julie held up her hand. "Say no more. I get it."

"Listen, can I call you sometime? Or I'll give you my number if that's better."

The corner of her mouth curled sweetly. "Sure. But not here."

My face went hot. "Look, if you don't want—"

"No, I mean, just don't give it to me right here. Date or no date, it would still be rude." She gave a quick glance around. "Leave it at the hostess desk."

I dared not move, still uncertain if she was serious or just trying to get rid of me. As if reading my thoughts, Julie grazed her hand over mine as she moved to walk away. She suddenly stopped and turned to me, whispering, "I promise I'll pick it up."

The rest of the evening was a delightful blur. I didn't mind *listening* to the radio girl talk for another hour. The table of women continued to carry on as I paid my check.

As I left the restaurant, I patted my jacket, ready to hand the valet my ticket. "Darn it, I forgot something. I'll be right back. Will you wait here for the car?"

I bolted straight for the hostess desk and scrawled my name and cell phone number on a cocktail napkin, along with, *I hope to hear from you soon.* I began to walk away, then came back and added my home and work numbers.

That night I paced my one-bedroom loft, wondering how long she would wait to call. If she would call at all. And what would I say? I'd not been serious about anyone, or even interested in anyone, for a long time. I went over a thousand conversations we might have, rehearsing them to see how I might sound. By the time sleep hit me, I was exhausted and had declared myself a conversational moron. Not that she was calling anyway.

Morning rolled in with its usual delicacy. After a late start that included three nicks of my neck and one shirt change after spilled coffee, I grabbed my coat from the wall hook and my keys from the side table, then sprinted to the door.

My land line rang.

I paused long enough to assume it was my office checking in before running out the door.

Later that evening I went straight home, opting out of the customary post-trading beer with friends. Absently, I hit the message button on my phone and went to the bedroom to pull on my favorite shabby running shorts and T-shirt.

Her voice sent me reeling back to the phone.

"Hi, Adam. It's Julie. I told you I'd pick up your number."

I could hear her smile, and it made my leg muscles weak all over again. I lay down on the couch, closed my eyes, and let thoughts of Julie overtake me as she continued.

"I hope you had a lovely remainder of your non-date date. So, um"—she chuckled—"if you happen to be free tomorrow evening…"

I listened to the message four more times, finally writing down her number. I did not delete the message.

Three hours later we were still on the phone, speaking in hushed and confidential tones though we were alone in our own apartments.

We'd spent the first hour on niceties, describing where we lived, what our jobs were, and running through our daily routines.

Julie was a child psychologist with her own private practice. Twice a week she volunteered at inner-city elementary schools, mostly serving children in the rough projects of Cabrini Green that could not afford counseling for their students. These children, she said, needed counseling more than anyone. She must live the same way her voice sounded, like a gentle, rolling wave.

I wished for another version of me to share. One that included volunteering, helping the homeless or disabled, anything altruistic. Anything other than what I truly did. To my surprise, she thought my work was fascinating and asked endless questions about the futures market and how the whole trading process worked on the floor, with a hundred men communicating by way of screams and thrashing arms.

I had known Julie for only an hour and already, just by listening to her, she made me want to be a better person.

Our second hour had been filled with stories of childhood, our neighborhoods, the friends and nemeses of our school days, and the many joys and regrets that accumulate over time. By the third hour, the conversation was peppered with exclamations of, "Oh man, I loved" insert movie or song or city, and "You, too?" A bond was taking shape, one more powerful in those three hours than I had formed during any former relationship.

The phone call turned into dinner, dinner turned into nightly dinners, which turned into sleeping over and, seamlessly, Julie became my girlfriend. Four years later, she became my wife. And somewhere between a phone call and *I do*, she became my lifeline.

After years of migrating, I took root for the first time. I called Chicago my home. We made friends, went to dinner, art gallery openings, wedding celebrations. We were young, free, and a vital part of the city's beating heart. We pompously discussed foreign films, but all secretly loved romantic comedies. We took turns cooking lavish dinners for each other, ending our feast- and wine-filled evenings with laughter, bravado, and board games. The group became my family, with Julie square in the middle.

Time passed quickly, smooth as a silk ribbon. And with that time, the couples in my large family began smaller families of their own. Movie nights were replaced with baby showers, dinners out became take-out and pizza delivery, our meals marked by early departures for toddlers' bedtimes.

Julie and I would arrive, diaper-bag-free, stroller-free, baby-free. And for a moment I would forget what the evening ahead would hold, instead expecting my group of the past: Loud. Trendy. Cutting edge.

We would walk into our friends' brownstones and reality would hit. The smell of baby lingered in the air, a mixture of lotion, breast milk, and diapers. Their clothes would inevitably be smeared with spit-up or creamy mashed peas. Discussions no longer circled around the latest installation at the modern art museum or an ad presentation gone awry at the NBC studio. Instead, talk amounted to comparing pediatricians and what vaccines were suddenly dangerous, or the amazement of having to go through an interview process for a preschool.

I found myself shrinking away from it all, repulsed. But not Julie. She'd soak in every word on parenting, take mental notes on what hospital gave the best care during childbirth and what new minivans had the highest safety rating. I'd physically pull back when asked if I'd like to hold a newborn. I did not. I was frightened to hold something so fragile, so vulnerable. But more than that, I was afraid of what emotions I might find in myself. I'd hear my friends declare they would die for their children, that they could never have imagined loving someone with such ferocity. The thought terrified me.

I'd sit in a side chair, away from the circle surrounding whatever baby had been introduced into our friends' lives, while Julie would get as close as possible, the first to hold the bundle. She would coo at it, rock, inhale the scent off its head. And when she politely passed the baby on to the next person, I'd see her eyes follow, sad and full of longing.

But not once during those years did she criticize or make me feel guilty. She loved me and she knew me, choosing not to expose my vulnerability, but instead protecting my fears. It was out of love that she put my needs in front of hers. It was a selfish need of mine, to love Julie and no other, and I knew it.

We experienced the normal ups and downs of marriage, but I never doubted that Julie was the person I was supposed to be with. She was my lover; she was my supporter; she was my best friend.

She made the wounds of my childhood heal into pale and indistinct scars.

Or so I believed.

૭

I ROLLED OUT of bed and grabbed my mug. "More coffee?"

"Listen to this one: Golden retriever puppies for sale. Cost of shots and registration only."

I leaned against the doorframe. "That's a tough one. Not much to work with. Puppies, shots, registration. I give up, what's the real story?"

Julie's face softened, then turned sadly still. "No. No story. It's only…puppies."

She sat motionless, looking down at the newsprint. Not looking at me. Not speaking. I scratched my thigh below my boxers, waiting. This was a typical standoff, both of us proficient in the arts of negotiation and war. The first to move or speak loses. I sighed with defeat, the flashing image of a puppy thumping through our hallways making me smile against my will.

"Maybe you should tear that one out. We have a free afternoon. It wouldn't hurt to see the litter."

Julie looked up slowly, her eyes watery. "I don't want a puppy."

She caught me mid-chuckle. "But then why—"

"I want a baby, Adam."

My body filled with lead as I slumped onto the couch. I wasn't going anywhere soon.

"Let's get a puppy first."

"No."

"I'm not ready. I want substantial savings put aside first. Kids are expensive. I want to move to a bigger place. You and I drive two-seaters, so that means a new car. And with your job, you're never home before seven. I'm usually later."

Tears welled in Julie's eyes. "Stop. It's not any of that and you know it. It's not the house or the savings. I want a baby. I've always wanted a baby. I told you I wanted babies before we got married. You told me it sounded great."

"It does sound great." I didn't sound convincing, not even to myself.

"What is it?" she asked.

"What?"

"The change. Why the change?"

"What change?"

"Goddammit. Don't jerk me around," she cried. "Why don't you want kids anymore?"

"I do want kids. Just not right now."

Julie crawled to the edge of the bed, pleading. "I'll be thirty-two this year, Adam. You'll be thirty-nine. If we wait any longer—"

"One year, maybe two. It won't matter—"

"We don't even know how long it will take for us to get pregnant. What if—"

"So what if it takes a while?"

"I don't want to be a sixty-year-old when our child graduates—"

"You won't be."

Our voices escalated despite attempting to swallow our respective frustrations.

"And I don't want just one baby. I want two or three."

"Three?"

"Yes, three. I've said that from the start. This isn't new information." Julie's voice caught in her throat. "And what if we can't conceive at all? Then we've wasted time we could have spent working on adoption—"

"I'm not going to adopt."

"But even if—"

"I don't want to raise a kid that's not mine."

"That's a horrible—"

"Horrible what?" I yelled. "You wouldn't know where the kid came from. It could be drug-addicted, genetically compromised, mentally unstable—"

"Agencies have records. Adoption is not a random—"

"This is ridiculous. We're fighting over hypothetical…"

Julie's eyes turned cold. Her pointed stare stopped me mid-sentence. "My wanting a baby is not hypothetical. And we're not fighting." She turned to the wall, and, for a moment, I thought the battle was over. I thought she'd unleash a fury of tears that would dry as she let me comfort her. She would cry the fight out of her, we would embrace, make love, hold each other, then go about the rest of our Sunday.

But she lifted her head with a calm that, for reasons unknown, made me shiver. She stood and silently pulled on a pair of jeans that had been draped over her reading chair.

As Julie brushed by me, I reached out for her elbow, a second too late. "Where are you going?"

"I'm going to get myself a puppy."

The puppy, Lola, came home with loppy ears, gigantic paws, and a mouth of tiny razors. She made us happy. I assumed, foolishly, that Lola would dissolve the thundercloud that menaced our marriage.

As Lola grew, Julie's attention was increasingly focused on walks, grooming, ear scratching, and baby talk. The golden retriever had become her priority. As I had secretly feared, if she had someone else to care for, she no longer needed to care for me.

Six months to the day after she brought Lola home, I found Julie at the kitchen table, staring into space. The air didn't feel right.

She calmly turned to me. "Can we talk?"

"Sure."

"I want a baby, Adam."

"We just got Lola."

"Lola is not a baby. You said we should get a dog first. I did. Now I want a baby."

Heat rose around my collar. I unbuttoned it.

"You planned this? From the time you brought Lola home?"

"I planned to have a baby with my husband."

I fought the pain shooting through my middle and the air leaving my lungs. "Who else would it be with?"

Her voice was low and cold. "I turned thirty-two last month. My time is precious. I won't give you any more of it unless we are moving forward together. And that means a baby."

"Are you threatening me?"

"No. It's just the way it is."

Julie stood, and I saw the large suitcase behind her chair. She took Lola's leash from the wall and clipped it to her collar. The dog jumped enthusiastically at the chance of a walk. "I rented a studio apartment in Bucktown. It's a month-to-month."

I sat in silence, staring at a blank spot on the wall as my lifeline walked out the door.

૭

THOUGH ALREADY TIRED, a deeper fatigue settled over me as I sat in the doctor's office. The public unveiling of our story—to hear myself say it out loud—made it real. I wasn't ready to deal with real. But my reality was getting worse by the day.

Dr. Marchand took a long breath and let it out slowly. "Adam, I think it's time you revisit your past."

"Theoretically?" I asked, hopeful.

The doctor smiled sympathetically.

"No. Literally. I think it would help you to go back. You need to face and work through, *really* work through, all the events you experienced at the lake. Your issues with commitment, fear of loving and losing again, all of it is connected to that summer. So, if you feel your marriage is worth saving and you truly want to say you gave everything you could, you have to begin at the source. You can't move forward without taking that first step."

I left the brownstone and started my slow walk home, head swimming.

Maybe it was time. Time for growth, as Dr. Marchand said. Time to move into another phase of adulthood, one in which you stop making excuses for the regrets lodged in your heart. I'd told him it sounded like he thought I should settle down, start a family, do what's expected. He'd nodded, then smiled. "And hopefully you'll do it without throwing yourself into a full-blown panic attack."

Certain memories scratched inside my chest, haunting me, whispering *let me out* until I couldn't ignore them. Dr. Marchand was right. It was time to exorcise those memories.

I made it to my front door before turning around and hurrying to my Porsche Turbo parked at the curb. Before I could change my mind, I started the engine and, within minutes, found myself northbound on Interstate 94.

SEVEN HOURS LATER, I slowed and turned onto Black Bear Lake Road. Time stopped. The rural Wisconsin road stretched for what seemed an eternity. I desperately wanted to turn my car around, but the lake drew me closer. I kept driving.

From the top of a long driveway, I looked down over the compound. Surprisingly, the lodge and grounds were just how I remembered them. The low-hanging fog likely masked some of the wear and weathering, but I had expected more decay, for the area to look like it had been abandoned for as long as I'd been away. Jack Pines—some of the worst trees on Earth with their scraggly limbs, my mother used to tell me—made up most of the forest surrounding the camp. As I scanned the expanse, they faded in and out of the background, as if God had become a discouraged artist, smearing his latest sketch in disgust.

Spring had been wet with unexpected bursts of warmth, a preview of the steamy summer ahead. The trees were fuller and greener than the usual late May foliage. As a child, the woods had been a magical fortress that enchanted me. As an adult staring into the buzzing, dark sea of bramble, all I felt was claustrophobic and afraid.

The lodge loomed ominously over the fourteen surrounding cabins, a stout schoolmarm guarding her charges. I pulled my car closer and as the tires hit gravel, my teeth clenched at the sound, reminiscent of bones being crushed. I rolled my window up.

As I stepped onto the lodge's long porch, my gaze fell on the lake, smooth as glass and surrounded by silence. I couldn't remember seeing it so still and, for a moment, I felt peace. I stepped tentatively from the porch to the blue stone walkway that tracked the line of cabins, cracked and crumbling like a disjointed spider web as it wove its way deep into the forest.

Of course, those cracks in the stone were nothing new. They were created long ago, during my last summer in Wisconsin.

My last summer at Black Bear Lake.

Chapter 2

AUGUST 1983

O ur station wagon, a worn pea-green Plymouth, crawled up Highway 94. Dad's compulsion to stick to the speed limit made the six-hour trip feel like a lifetime. Donna Summer bellowed from the radio and, unbelievably, Mom drowned her out with her rendition of *She Works Hard for the Money*. Feigning shock, Dad asked if we'd accidently hit a cat. Mom punched his arm with a laugh and continued to sing, even louder, directly in his ear. With the windows rolled down, her light auburn curls danced around her pale face.

I held a coveted spot in the back seat beside the door and closed my eyes against the warm August air flooding in. Kevin, the middle brother, mirrored my position. Youngest of all was Mikey, who sat squashed between us, bellowing in protest. The battle between Mikey and Kevin repeatedly escalated and abated, not unlike major nations fighting over land.

"Get your sweaty legs away from mine!"

"You're the sweaty one. You look like a pig."

"You smell like a pig."

"Because I'm sitting next to you, dweeb!"

While Dad shot empty threats over his shoulder, my almost-fifteen-year-old mind drifted home. Home to my friends I wasn't with and the parties I would miss. To swimming pools alive with smooth, tanned bodies, thrashing through the heavily chlorinated water like slippery minnows. To the limbs tangled unintentionally—and sometimes very intentionally—beneath the surface. To the girls discovering the power of bikinis, and me discovering how powerless I was around them.

I had decided this would be my summer. Rather than bury my nose in poetry books at the library, I was going to venture out, do all the things my friends did. I'd have the same memories and stories to laugh at next school year. But June came and went. Then July followed, and all I had accomplished during *my summer* was railing against the numerous family outings forced on me. In my parents' minds we should've been glued, one unmoving unit enjoying every second of life together as though it were a gift. But as the farmhouses, tractors, and cows flew past me, my resentment grew. The familiar anger at being ripped away from my inspired summer plans, of being held captive in the wagon and the destination that lay ahead, roiled just under the surface. Despite failing to reach any of my social goals for the summer, the endless possibility of hope clung to my pubescent brain, telling me, *I could if only...*

A small corner of my mind knew I should enjoy these moments with my family. With my mother. I should catalogue every conversation, every stitch of laughter, every warm embrace in her arms. But that corner was closed off and locked away. The reality was simply too painful to consciously consider. The easier course was irritation and anger.

I pulled out my spiral pocket notebook and flipped it open, scanning the entries, which had grown darker over the summer. I scribbled, pressing too hard. *How can a phoenix burn and rise again when it's never allowed to fly in the first place?* I stared at the words and nodded with satisfaction. The notebook had been a gift from my mother. She had slipped it into my hand one day after returning from the grocery store. "For the words when they come to you." My parents, both writers, were continual in their quiet celebration of my love of literature. If anyone of real literary knowledge had seen what I'd written, they would have scoffed with pity. But to myself, I was poet laureate.

Kevin peered at my writing over Mikey's head. "Ooh la la. What are the flowers and butterflies and grasshoppers doing today?"

Mikey laughed and chimed in. "Yeah! And lovebirds!"

"Shut up, idiots." I shoved the notebook between the seat and car door.

Kevin laughed. "Dude, you are the biggest fairy."

My arm shot out and, in one swift movement, smacked Kevin and Mikey. The stillness that followed seemed endless but lasted only seconds. Two quiet beats before Mikey started to wail. Kevin, trying to punch me in retaliation, missed and hit Mikey again. Mom turned to us with a furrowed brow and reprimands on her lips, but Dad put his hand around her shoulder and smiled. As I ducked, missing another of Kevin's swings, my eyes fell on Black Bear Lake.

We had arrived.

The fence at the outer perimeter of the drive had been repainted a dazzling white with stone pillars erected on each side of the entrance. The back seat wars forgotten, we clambered to the car's windows and stuck our heads outside, sucking in the Northwoods air. Our sweaty thighs squeaked across the leather seats. We pulled at the Izod tennis shirts sticking to our backs, anticipating the cool lake water on our skin.

The wagon rolled to a stop next to a long line of travel-weary cars. They were thick with dust and dirt, representing the miles each had traveled to get to the lake. The cars would sit covered in mud, happily ignored for the next month.

Kevin and I tumbled out before Dad could cut the engine. Mikey was still fumbling with his seat belt when we spied Grannie shuffling toward us across the lodge porch.

"There they are!" The explosive Italian voice sang out, amplified by her late-afternoon chardonnay. "My sweets. My sweets." Her thick, doughy arms enveloped me and my brothers, blanketing us with Aqua Net hairspray and Caleche perfume.

We were suffocating blissfully when the roaring hordes of relatives descended on us. To keep the many cousins straight, we had labeled them by age. Born within a four-year span, the college-aged cousins were the Feathers. All of them, even the boys, had adopted the feathered hairstyle the moment it became popular. Kevin's group of same-age cousins were called the Means, originally because they fell smack in the middle of our generation. Father started the nickname as a thinking man's joke. As they grew older, the name became increasingly appropriate, though they weren't so much mean as obnoxious. The youngest group was, by far, the largest and were aptly named the Minnows, little bodies bobbing in the lake from sun-up to sundown.

They swarmed toward us, all our bright-blonde and rich brown-haired family members, every faction of the family represented and each speaking louder than the next.

"Sarah!"

"How was the trip?"

"You must be exhausted."

"When you guys get in?"

"Have you talked to Daddy yet? Well, don't. He's in a state."

"Kevin! Hey Kevin!"

"Mikey, put on your trunks. We're building a sand fort!"

"You like those tires? Did you notice a difference on the highway?"

"Oh, I love your new haircut."

"Mamma, what's wrong with Daddy?"

"Adam, Dannie is up unpacking."

"Anybody see Old Papa yet?"

"Oh, you know him. If he's not in a tizzy about one thing…"

"So, did Ron end up coming?"

"Kids, don't run off without your bags."

"How are you feeling?"

"Yeah, he's here. We'll talk."

"Are you ready for dinner?"

"Honey, go grab your brothers. They need to put their bags in the cabins."

"Mamma, dinner won't be ready for hours. The stove wasn't working."

"Don't let the dog jump in the car. He's all wet!"

"I'll take the bags up. They'll just get left out here if I don't."

"Oh, that's right. The gas company just left. Always something…"

"Come on Sarah. Let's grab a glass of wine and dodge Daddy."

I stayed by the car as the tornado of family and dogs twisted and sputtered its way to the lodge. Alone with the trees and a crying loon, I closed my eyes and held my face toward the late afternoon sun. When I opened them, I smiled at the shifting shadows of the Jack Pines, the shiny waves lapping at the edge of the lake, the distant laughter of my family, and the fresh smell of summer.

As quickly as I scooped up my bag to begin the uphill trek to my cabin—and to my Dannie—the far-fetched dreams of a life-changing summer, glistening girls, and all the imagined splendor of the city vanished in the Northwoods' air.

Chapter 3

A symphony of crying toddlers, barking dogs, suitcase zippers, and children calling in search of misplaced swimsuits floated out from the various cabins I passed while running to the top of the blue stone pathway. I did not stop to greet my extended family. I would have time later to answer questions about my schoolwork, my growth spurt, and whether I'd found a girlfriend. The only person I wanted to see was Dannie.

I flew across the stones two at a time, crashing full force into her cabin's screen door.

"Dannie!" I shielded my face against the thick mesh.

Uncle Ron shuffled to the door, disheveled and unshowered, wearing soiled cut-off shorts and an unbuttoned flannel shirt. "Hey Adam. Dannie went down to the lodge to find you." Ron turned and went back into the cabin without another word. His brusque demeanor barely registered, and I was immediately overtaken by disappointment.

I picked up my duffle and walked toward the boys' cabin which, along with the girls', had been built a few years prior to accommodate the growing families. By the end of the first day, they would resemble swarming beehives, teeming messes of cousins, brothers, and sisters, littered with sleeping bags, wet towels, six-packs of Tab, and bags of chips. I walked into the boys' cabin and inhaled the familiar smell of cedar planks. Homemade bunk beds lined the walls two feet apart, each with a set of fresh sheets and a wool plaid blanket. I was thrilled to claim the one in the back corner, the trophy bunk because its location gave me a means of defense against midnight raids by the girls. Worst was the front left, the first one people encountered as they entered the cabin. Trying to get any sleep there was annoying enough, but it was terrifying when black bears tried to break in after smelling our mess of popcorn and apple cores. I'd learned that lesson the previous summer.

I tossed my bag on the back bunk to mark my territory and began digging through the overstuffed duffle. I got down to the stack of swimwear that—in contrast to the many shirts and shorts that would go untouched over the coming month—would make up my daily uniform. I chose a pair of pricey trunks, an extravagant gift from Mom elicited by my incessant pleading. I begged for more than a month, secretly imagining myself at pool parties thrown by the most popular girls in school, surrounded by bowls of tortilla chips and pitchers of soft drinks. I dreamed often of the gatherings and even more frequently of the hosts. Smiling, I had tried on the new shorts, confident they guaranteed me a place in the elusive in-crowd. The familiar tug of anger began to pull at my stomach. Once again, a summer had gone by with no pool parties, no popular girls, no in-crowd carrying me through to the new school year. I shook off the feeling as best I could and pulled on the trunks.

Before I could tighten the drawstring, the cabin door flew open and a streak of blonde hair barreled toward me, knocking me onto the bunk. Dannie sat on top of me, straddling my stomach and pinning down my arms.

"What's buzzin' cuzzin?" Dannie was wearing her bathing suit, a fuchsia bikini with neon green triangles and yellow circles swirling over the fabric. Living in San Diego, she had a perpetual golden tan that magnified my milky Midwest pallor. I'd get some sun after a month at the lake, but it would begin to fade the moment September started.

Although we talked on the phone regularly, it had been two years since I'd seen Dannie in person. Her mother— Mom's third cousin—and Ron were having marital problems. When they stayed away the summer before, I suffered through the most boring August reunion I could remember.

I took her in for a split second. I'd seen her family Christmas photo that winter, but she seemed different just a few months later. Dannie's body was curvier, her eyes a sharper blue than I remembered, her smooth blonde hair falling almost to her narrow waist.

She had changed.

I bucked, knocking Dannie onto the next bed, both of us laughing with joy and relief to be in each other's company again.

"Come on. Let's go swim."

Dannie and I grew up with cousins who were either several years older or younger than we were. Feathers, Means, or Minnows.

In our family, we had only each other.

Chapter 4

annie and I shuffled down the pathway behind the lodge. The grass tapered off at the beach where children, like a colony of ants, bustled with focused determination as they played horseshoes and built sprawling sandcastles. Our aunts lazily supervised from their chaises, books propped open in their laps, absently calling for the children to be careful. Farther out, the older kids were a line of lemurs, running full speed and launching themselves from the dock into the lukewarm lake, taking in mouthfuls of water as they laughed.

Dannie threw her towel on a chair. "Let's get something to eat. I'm starving."

"Didn't your mom stock your fridge?" Each cabin was self-contained, as the children well knew. At the end of the month, we congregated at the cabin with the best uneaten snacks.

"I'm not in their cabin. I'm staying with the girls."

"You hate the bunkhouse."

"I know, but it's better than staying with my mom and dad."

Her tone kept me from saying more.

We walked down the stone pathway, past the beach. Two Feathers, Eric and Terry, were rolling a half-keg toward the sand, excited to take advantage of Wisconsin's lower legal drinking age. Doing their share of the work, fellow Feathers Angie and Paul were digging out a large pit not far from where we held the evening bonfires. They would bury the keg, the sand acting as a natural cooler, and leave only the pump and hose above ground during the night's festivities.

The lodge was loud, large, energetic, and overwhelming—much like our family. In the main living room, Michael Jackson pumped from an oversized boombox. One of the many summer babysitters sat on the floor, unenthusiastically coloring with a handful of five-year-olds fighting over a single blue crayon. We passed the saloon-style bar, long and lacquered and stocked full of countless evils the adults would enjoy during their stay.

Dannie had a gleam in her eye. "Wanna beer?"

"What? Um, no. My mom would kill me."

Dannie shrugged and kept walking toward the kitchen. As we went farther into the lodge, the sounds of kitchen chaos grew. Shrieks of laughter were drowned out by belly laughs. Adults tried to talk over one another while waves of enthusiastic shouting preceded exuberant backslapping. The aroma of the family meal enveloped us; it was the smell of our summers. Granny stood at the stove in one of her well-worn cotton lake dresses, one hand stirring a buttery, slow-cooking spaghetti sauce, the other holding her wine glass. Dannie's mom, Patty, had the same sun-streaked blonde hair as her daughter and wore it thrown in a loose ponytail. She and my mother stood side by side at the butcher block, hips touching as they peeled, scooped, and chopped cucumbers for our salad. Gramps's older sister, Genevieve, sat hunched over the long kitchen table, cane resting on her thigh, kneading the dough for her biscuits. They always turned out too dry and hard to eat, but no one had the heart to tell her. Aunt Tammy, tall and lean, came into the kitchen from the backyard, where she had been grilling bratwurst. The dense smells, mixing and swirling, were so strong my mouth immediately began to water.

Tammy slammed the tray of sausages onto the island counter, grinning amicably. "I'm of the personal opinion that any grilling should be done by the men of this family. I'm sweating like a pig out there."

"I'm of the opinion that I'd rather not have my brats turned into rubber, so the men grilling is not an option,"

Mom muttered loud enough to send the women into another fit of giggles. Noticing our arrival, she winked mischievously. "You weren't supposed to hear that. Don't tell your father."

"Your secret is safe with me. For a price." I reached for a brownie from the pile stashed in the corner. Grannie's head snapped up abruptly. "Not so fast, Mister. Here," she said gently, taking my elbow. "Try this. I just want to make sure it's all right." She scooped a large portion of her sauce into a love-worn wooden spoon and handed it to me, smiling softly. Dannie slid into place beside her mother and began peeling carrots.

I held the spoon at my mouth, blowing away the steam. As I watched the group of women, I felt an unfamiliar sting of jealousy. They danced around the kitchen, around each other, in a beautifully choreographed waltz that only they knew. Arms weaved above and below, reaching for salt, tomatoes, and lettuce. Hands nudged and patted hips to the side, out of the way of opening drawers and the hot oven door. They silently stroked a lock of hair or kissed a forehead when passing through the narrow aisle between the island and sink. They were their own clan, set apart from the boys and men. It was an intangible relationship. The weight and mass so undeniable, but at the same time so elusive it slipped through my fingers before I could grasp it. I watched my mom and ached for this bond with her.

"Well?" Grannie looked straight at me. Over the last few years, between my growing and her shrinking, we stood eye-to-eye.

"You don't even need the pasta," I said, slurping the last of the sauce. Grannie smiled widely as she patted my behind, shooing me away and humming a lilting old Italian love song her own mother once sang.

"Sweetheart," Mom said, "grab some more carrots from the fridge, please." She finished her cucumbers and threw the scraps into a bucket for feeding the pigs.

Caring for the Pig Bucket, a task assigned to the youngest cousins, was bittersweet. Every afternoon they would drag the heaping pale of leftovers and scraps to the prairie on the far side of the lake, where we kept a small pen with two

young swine. The Minnows, using their collective
manpower, would overturn the bucket then flee, screaming
with wild elation, feigning fear of an attack. Once safely
outside the fence, they dropped to the grass in uncontrolled
laughter, rolling into each other, snorting and grunting like
the animals they taunted. After the first year, we learned not
to name the pigs. No one ever got over the sight of Penelope
and Sweetpea roasting on a slow-turning spit.

I crossed to the fridge as Grannie turned to my mother.
"It's a hundred degrees in here, take off that sweater."
Tammy shot Mom a nearly imperceptible glance as Mom
looked at me, then silently returned to her vegetables. My
parents had decided not to tell Grannie or Gramps yet. The
fear being that at their age, the worry would be too much to
bear; the hope being that the chemo would eradicate my
mother's cancer and my grandparents would never have to
know. But the treatments hadn't worked.

"What was Daddy so agitated about?" Tammy asked,
smoothly changing the subject.

Granny, visibly frustrated, took a sip of wine, and her
Italian accent thickened. "He's fighting with the gas
company. The gas works, then it stops, then it works again.
Even early this morning the stove wouldn't light.
Fortunately, it started before Il Babbo came down for
breakfast. The bills have been through the roof this year, but
the company says it can't find a leak anywhere and we must
be using more than we realize. Babbo made the company
send its people out again yesterday before you arrived. They
checked every cabin and didn't come up with a thing. I will
say, you could smell gas. I couldn't put my finger on it at
first, but that's what it was, all right. But no, no, no, the gas
company wouldn't listen to any of that. Their gadgets didn't
pick it up, so they told Il Babbo he must be mistaken. You
know him, though. Not satisfied until he's proven right. And
until that happens, he will be an absolute bear."

The women chuckled again, chirping about Gramps's
past obsessions. They recounted his vast flower garden,
which took the caretakers and staff three long months to
plant and two short days to be consumed by deer. They
recalled the pond he had workers dig behind his cabin and

fill with bullfrogs, only to discover that their foghorn night songs attracted every otter within a ten-mile radius, all happy to graze on the unsuspecting prey. They laughed over the annual battle with the dock installers over the previous year's location, where it should be currently, and why the cost rose mysteriously every summer. None of Gramps's missions were ever taken seriously by the family. On the contrary, we waited in happy anticipation of his next entertaining venture.

"A bear to be around is right. He puts Old Papa to shame," Tammy laughed.

Dannie lit up. "Grannie, have you seen Old Papa yet this summer?"

"Heavens, yes. That old bear has us figured out so well, you'd think we called to let him know when we were arriving."

Old Papa was a local black bear, a titan the size of a Mack truck with an affinity for our compound. We believed an understanding existed between the two parties: We'd leave him be as he grazed our trashcan leftovers, so as long as he kept a respectable distance and pretended to be frightened when we spotted him.

"How old is he, do you think?"

"Goodness, Sarah was maybe five when he first started coming around." Grannie smiled fondly.

"Yes, I remember the first time I laid eyes on him out there." Mom gestured to the door behind her. "He looked like a dinosaur even then, he was so huge."

"Yeah, but nothing like he is now." Tammy laughed. "That old thing eats better than most people I know."

We often saw Old Papa after dark, lumbering to the back door of the lodge for his evening meal. We would see bears every year, but they would show themselves for a season, then migrate to safer cover. Old Papa, though terrifying in his size and apparent strength, had become a beloved fixture in our summer world.

"I think Daddy would win if it came down to a fight between the two." Tammy winked at me. "And I would pay a hefty price for a front-row ticket."

Tammy was three years younger than my mother, though no one would ever guess. She and Mom were polar opposites. But, instead of their differences causing friction, the women were like puzzle pieces—different in every way yet inexplicably fitting perfectly together. While Mom was small-boned and fine-featured, seemingly frail in body and voice, Tammy was athletic and bold. Her sculpted muscles and booming voice overtook any room, filling it with energy and light. Mom would happily stand on the sidelines at a party, content to watch the action from afar, relishing some small talk with one or two close companions. Tammy would stand squarely in the middle of the crowd, head thrown back in a boisterous laugh, and leave the event with twenty more friends than when she arrived.

Despite their differences, the sisters relied on each other. They shared their most intimate troubles and guarded their secrets from outsiders. They seemed to communicate by an electrified wire tethering them to each other yet invisible to others. They clung together in childhood and adolescence to defend against a domineering father and alcoholic mother. They protected each other through the ups and downs of their marriages, the anxieties of childrearing and the uncertainties of growing older. Mom, through her quiet introspection, gave Tammy safety and security. Tammy threw my mother into situations she would never venture into on her own, forcing Mom to experience life and find unexpected joy.

Grannie shook her head slowly, her white bun shifting gently to one side. "Bear fight or not, the gas company said we have to do a complete overhaul next spring. I don't have it in me to come a month early just to hear your babbo grumble and protest."

Without looking up from her salad preparation, Dannie's mother quietly offered her husband's help. "Maybe Ron could come help manage the project. Be the eyes for Gramps. Make sure the gas company does a thorough job."

"Why on earth would he want to do that?"

"Work is work, Grannie."

"Oh, he makes plenty. No need to leave fish for fish."

"It's just"—Patty swallowed hard—"he hasn't been working much."

Grannie stopped stirring and looked steadily at Patty. "Why's that, now? We're in the middle of a building boom. I don't see any shortage of construction jobs."

Mom's cousin kept her eyes on the chopping block. "Ron might have fallen out of good graces with his union leader."

"How long has he been loafing this time?"

"Long enough," Patty said softly.

"And I suppose he's helping out around the house, fixing meals, making himself useful?" The silence that followed was answer enough. "I didn't think so."

Mom gave Grannie a level glance. "Be nice."

Grannie turned back to her pot with a huff. "Zebras don't change their stripes, do they?"

Gramps's older sister twisted a juice glass into the flattened dough, making a round puck that would become one of her inedible biscuits. "I think it's a great idea, him coming up to work," Genevieve said. "Put some extra food on your table. Plus, it would give you an excuse to send him off for a while. If you won't leave him, at least give yourself a break from that womanizing deadbeat."

Mom sighed. "Good Lord."

"Aunt Gennie, just make your damn biscuits," Tammy snapped.

Dannie's eyes flickered, and the women's waltz began again, bodies moving around each other, pushing the scene in the direction they want it to go, just as a leading dancer rhythmically moves his partner.

"Did you remember to put in the baking soda?" Tammy asked Genevieve, a bit too loudly. "You don't want the kids using them for skipping stones again."

Genevieve laughed and smacked Tammy with her walking stick. "Wicked girl."

"Pour me another, would you, Patty?" Grannie held out her white wine glass. Patty, tears in her eyes, silently took the glass to the bar.

Mom smiled at me, the one that was no smile at all. I knew this look. It was not happiness. It was not contentment. It was just the opposite and it said, *All is not well but we can't talk about it at this moment. Just smile for now.* "Sweetheart, why don't you and Dannie go out back and see which activity you've been assigned."

"Don't wander too far, you love birds," Genevieve sang, winking affectionately.

Since we were babies, Dannie and I had endured taunting from our aunts, uncles, and, at times, our own parents regarding our closeness. At the lightest of times we would hear, "Aren't they adorable together?" The worst went something like, "You know, if you weren't cousins, you would be the perfect couple." We learned that the more we denied and fought their humorous accusations, the worse the attacks became. We developed deaf ears.

I grabbed an apple from the fruit bowl, trying to appease my insatiable teenage appetite. "Come on." As we left the kitchen, I caught Dannie throwing Aunt Genevieve a steely look.

The large dry-erase board, which listed all the activity assignments for the cousins, showed Dannie and I leading the summer's volleyball tournament. We groaned, knowing we would have to pull together teams and a schedule. Just pulling enough people away from vodka lemonades and shaded lawn chairs sometimes took half a day. But before that hurdle was the detestable task of assembling the equipment. We walked to the shed at the far side of the yard to take inventory. We pulled the rusty but usable poles and flung limp volleyballs onto the grass. Dannie groaned as she dragged out the spider web of net.

"It'll take us the whole month just to untangle this mess. Why can't people roll it up when they put it away?"

"Because by the time they put all the equipment away, they're so sick of volleyball they never want to see it again."

We both stood and stared at the impossible ball of rope.

"Come on," I said. "Let's just do it." I sat on the grass and started at one end. Dannie sighed heavily and slumped next to me, pulling the other end into her lap.

"I hate volleyball."

I grinned. "What're you talking about? You love volleyball. Your team wins every year. I don't think that's a coincidence, Miss California Outdoors Girl." I shoved her with my shoulder, but she remained somber.

"It's a stupid game and I'm tired of it. We should do something new this year."

"Like what?"

"Like anything."

"Like *what*?"

"*Anything*." Never had I heard such a hard edge in her voice. I fell into silence as we continued to unravel the net.

I waited for Dannie to speak first, to apologize, but she stayed under her dark cloud, lost to me. I stewed with indignant resentment. Without Dannie as a partner, I felt alone and isolated, forced to spend my summer hours untangling a net that no one would appreciate. I sat, steaming, sweat beading on my forehead, wondering what I was missing in the city and what fun my friends were surely having. My mind drifted to a girl at home. Tessa, from second semester history class. Tessa had never barked at me or given me the silent treatment like Dannie. Tessa sat directly behind me and fired flirty missiles at her willing target. Her toes caressed the backs of my calves, her fingers wove through the hair on the back of my head, and her tantalizing whispers floated to my ears. Tessa, a petite brunette, was a junior varsity cheerleader who might grow up to be squat, wide-hipped, suburban soccer mom. But as a teen, she was alluringly muscular and well-endowed.

When I realized I could reciprocate the flirtation, Tessa and I spent months practicing sexual innuendo and physical maneuvering on each other. It was all new and tantalizingly provocative after growing up in a household where affection was promoted but sex was taboo. Tessa was a foreign planet to explore. Our exchanges grew in frequency and intensity. But before I knew it, the school year ended and so did my lukewarm forays in sexual experimentation. I kept thinking of all the risks I wished I'd taken with her, playing out new scenes in my mind, where my fear didn't get the best of me. I found myself obsessed with the thought of Tessa being at one of our classmates' pool parties. *If she had been, I wouldn't have known*, I thought. I had been so close, only to end the school year with no experience.

While Dannie worked, I stared at the volleyball netting. It made me feel empty, like a well running bone dry.

Gnats swarmed our bodies. I tried to inhale small sniffs of air to keep them from flying into my mouth. Dannie swatted at a cluster. I smacked my thigh where the no-see-ums had begun to bite and finally surrendered to the heavy silence.

"They were really bad last year, too. The bugs."

Dannie gave a small smile and glanced up. "Really?"

I let out my breath. We were okay again, for now, but I'd never needed to censor myself with Dannie. This was new territory. Uncomfortable territory. I wasn't sure how to navigate it, so I remained cautious.

"Yeah," I said. "And the biting flies, too. Something to do with all the rain. It'll probably be the same at home since it was pretty much raining all last month."

"I can't imagine spending summer in the rain."

"*Like totally, for sure.*" I smirked. Dannie punched my arm.

"I wondered how long it would be before you started. We don't all sound like Valley Girl."

"Totally?"

"I'm so sure!"

Dannie laughed deeply and hit me again. As quickly as it had darkened, the light in her eyes reappeared. "Hey, I made you a tape."

"Really?"

"Yeah. I was bummed out that we didn't come last summer, so all this year when I heard a song that reminded me of you, I'd add it. I listen to it all the time and can always imagine us sitting around the bonfire singing. *Jack and Diane, Edge of Seventeen, Every Little Thing She Does Is Magic*…"

"*Sexual Healing*?" I blurted out. We fell into each other, laughing. I began singing. Dannie tried to stop me, but eventually gave in and belted out with me, "And when I get that feeling, I need—"

I stopped mid-sentence as baby Tommy, our four-year-old cousin, streaked by completely naked, white-blond hair flying behind him. His entrance, however, was not what startled me. Tommy was loved for his carefree exhibitionism, making it acceptable for other toddlers to flaunt their bodies on the beach.

What caught my attention was the person following him.

She moved like liquid. A mane of amber hair rolled over her bare shoulders and down her back in waves. She nimbly maneuvered around other children; her attention focused solely on Tommy as he dove headfirst into the sand on the volleyball court. He rolled and writhed, filling his crevices with grains and embedding the sand so deeply in his scalp it would take the rest of the summer to wash out. The girl stopped, looked at Dannie and me, and sighed. She glanced at Tommy, deciding he was content for the moment before approaching us, body bouncing with every step. Her red bikini bottom rode dangerously low and her triangle top shifted slightly, allowing me to glimpse a pink rose. I'd never seen a real tattoo up close and it captivated me, my eyes unable to meet hers as she introduced herself.

"Hi. I'm Amy."

"Danielle."

"Um. Adam."

"Can I sit with you guys? I think Tommy's going to be here a while." She glanced behind her as a group of our young cousins worked enthusiastically to bury Tommy in a sandy coffin.

I realized Amy was staring at me staring at her tattoo, while Dannie stared at us both. I refocused on a small knot in the rope resting on my lap. Amy sat next to me, leaning back on her elbows and stretching her legs to full length.

"That's quite a mess you have there." Amy smiled broadly.

"Yeah, we've got to get it undone today. The tournament starts tomorrow." I chanced a glance in Amy's direction and found she was still grinning at me.

"Volleyball tournament? I love volleyball."

"You should sign up to play."

"I don't know." Amy looked at Tommy again. Only his head was visible above ground. "I'm babysitting for Kelly and Mark this summer, and they haven't exactly been gracious with time off during the day, you know? They come up here for a month-long family vacation then panic when they have to spend five minutes alone with him. Sometimes I wonder why they even had Tommy."

Mark worked as an advertiser in downtown Chicago. He left the house as the sun came up and stayed out after work with the other *ad-men* until Tommy was long asleep. Kelly was a full-time Junior League volunteer and lady-who-lunched. But the time she spent helping underprivileged kids left little for her own. I thought of my parents. Both my father, a psychology professor at the University of Chicago, and my mother, a florist who taught evening writing classes for seniors at a local community center, always found enough time for their children.

Amy looked at us, pained. "Oh man, I'm sorry. That was really uncool. I mean, it's your family. I shouldn't have said that. I'm sure they love Tommy a lot."

"No prob." I smiled reassuringly, fixing my gaze on her eyes a second too long. Or maybe just long enough to realize I liked her. *Really* liked her. My face burned in the same uncontrollable way it did when Tessa first leaned forward in class and whispered in my ear.

I cleared my throat. "Where are you from? Do you live near Mark and Kelly?"

"No. My dad went to college with one of Mark's friends. They all met up years ago for a Cubs game and have been friends since. Beer, hot dogs, and baseball are kind of bonding that way. So, when I was looking for a summer job, my dad put the word out. Mark suggested I stay with them and watch Tommy. Guess their normal girl needed an extended break." She winked at me, causing my knee to shake. "I actually live closer to downtown."

A jolt surged through me. "Really? Me too. Where do you live?"

"Bucktown."

"I'm in Hyde Park."

"That's a nice area."

"Thanks. How's Bucktown?"

"Okay, I guess. It's just my dad and me, and we move a lot. Pretty much every place is the same."

"Where's your mom?"

"She and my dad split up when I was six."

I thought of my parents again and our tight-knit nucleus. "And you stayed with your dad?"

"Yeah, he was definitely the better choice. I never even hear from my mom anymore."

"That's got to be weird."

Amy shrugged. "Not too bad. My dad is a chef and the restaurant lets me work there part-time during the school year, so, we get to spend a lot of time together. He makes up for my mom being such a bitch."

My eyes widened. I had been around a lot of swearing by my friends, and at times I'd overheard my father's students engage in tirades of profanity. But the way Amy used that word to describe her own mother, the way it rolled off her tongue, was jarring. I looked to Dannie to see if she shared my shock, but she just fiddled with the netting in her lap, disengaged, as if we weren't even there.

At first, I was too flustered to respond. When it hit that Amy's edginess intrigued me, I was more rattled. I didn't want to say anything that might stop our conversation; I wanted to impress her with a clever remark, to seem as mysterious to her as she was to me.

Then Dad came around the corner.

"Ah, so this is where the pool of teenage hormones went."

"Dad!" My insides curdled.

"Hello, we haven't met yet. I'm John, Adam's father."

Amy jumped up and gave Dad a hug, his surprise visible. "Hi. I'm Amy. I'm babysitting Tommy this summer for Angela and Mark."

Dad's head tilted slightly, a curious look on his face. "I'm, uh, heading to the Corner Store for some fishing bait." He turned his focus to me. "I came to see if you wanted to go, but now I won't bother." He winked at me, then grinned while lifting his eyebrows. I felt nauseous.

As Dad walked away, I turned to make sure Dannie shared my humiliation, but was left wanting.

Dannie was gone.

Chapter 5

That evening I wove my way through a throng of relatives, all freshly scrubbed for dinner. They carried plates piled high with salad, sausages, and Grannie's special pasta that we would eat all month long without growing tired of it.

I had chosen the right shirt and even snuck a handful of gel from Mom's bathroom. My hair was slicked to the side and my collar stood at attention as I scanned the large dining hall for Amy. My head was still swiveling when a hip checked mine, sending me crashing into Kevin and the other Means.

"Hey bro! What's your problem?" Kevin asked in his thickest Sean Penn voice. Since last summer, the Means had morphed into Jeff Spicoli clones, pseudo beach bums ready to catch a wave on their imaginary surfboards.

"Ah man." I tried wiping bratwurst grease off the bottom of my shorts and whipped around, ready to pummel one or more of the reckless twelve-year-olds. Instead I found Dannie, hands on her weaponized hips, smirking.

"I was going to put you on my volleyball team, but now I'm rethinking it, klutz."

I raised an eyebrow. "I thought you hated volleyball. You said it was stupid and we should find something else."

"Yeah, yeah. I was in a bad mood."

"Really? I hadn't noticed."

"Aunt Gennie pissed me off, smartass."

"Takes one to know one."

Dannie smiled wide. "Come on, let's go scarf."

We tacked ourselves to the end of the never-ending buffet line, sighing with self-pity.

"Where did you go today?" I asked.

"For a swim and then back to the bunkhouse." Dannie craned her neck to see how much food was left on the table. I scanned the room again. No Amy.

"I untangled the rest of the net."

"Nice."

"Thought maybe you could *help* and we could string it up in the morning?"

"Why don't you ask Amy?"

"Who?" My face burned.

Dannie turned to me, her eyes squared with mine. "I get it. She's way hot."

I couldn't breathe. Even if I could find words to argue, Amy's sexual energy was indisputable. Dannie bumped me with her shoulder, nudging me forward in line. "It's cool. Don't have a cow."

"Let's go, guys," Tammy said. "Keep it moving." She hustled people through the long line, doling out sausages with one hand and grilled sweet peppers with the other. Dannie and I made our dinners and headed for the dining hall. I spied my mother sitting alone at a table.

"Well hello there, beautiful lady. Is this seat taken?" I asked, giving her a flirtatious wink. My mood had improved tremendously since encountering Amy. I plopped down my plate clumsily, spilling slices of pepper on the table. Mom picked them up absently, slowly placing them one by one on the rim.

"Hello, sweetheart. You two have a good day?"

Dannie slid into the chair opposite mine. "Yeah, it was excellent. How was yours?"

"Very nice. In the kitchen all day. It's amazing how fast the hours fly by when you're with people you love." Her languid tone would make most people think she was deeply relaxed and content, but I knew she was just exhausted.

Dannie took a sip of her water, nodding in pleasant agreement.

I started to stand. "Want me to get you a plate?"

"No, no. Your father is getting one for me. Thank you, love."

Over the last year, my mind had begun to play games, ignoring the overt signs that reminded me she was sick. If I didn't recognize it, it wasn't happening, and life could go on as normal. Recently, though, the reminders were coming so frequently my brain couldn't dissolve reality fast enough. I didn't want to see her shaking chills and fatigue. Her distracted looks when she'd return after a doctor's appointment. Mom's body was failing, yet she was only willing to show a grateful smile. I wanted her to boss us around. I wanted her to be irritable and mean and angry, to snap at me so I'd have a reason to let out my tears. She asked me for nothing, and I could do nothing to help—not even get her a plate of food when she was too tired to carry it herself. Small moments like these roiled inside me and were almost worse than the initial blow of finding out she was sick.

Mom placed her hand on mine and smiled. Her eyes said, *I know, I know.*

Dad returned, two plates and two glasses precariously balanced between his forearms. I grabbed one of each and set them in front of Mom. Dad plopped down his dinner and drink, then rumpled my hair. I etched the moment in my mind, holding the scene of perfect normalcy in my heart like a delicate snow globe, then willed the mind game of nothing-is-wrong to return. Everything was okay. It was just Mom, Dad, and me sitting down to dinner at Black Bear Lake.

My daydream was interrupted when the sound of clinking glass reverberated through the dining hall, culminating in a tidal wave crescendo. Gramps strode regally from around the corner, his scotch held high. The family roared as they beat fists on tables and rhythmically stomped the floor. "Gramps! Gramps! Gramps!" The noise was deafening. Gramps took in every cheer, whoop, and holler the same way a dehydrated dog would lap up water.

His thick Polish voice boomed over the crowd, affected words sprinkled with dramatic pause. He made no motion for the affectionate crowd to cease.

"Tonight…we come together as a family. Not as separate clans joined by a proud lineage…but as one!"

We clapped madly.

"We come together…where we have for decades past…in the spirit of love…and heritage."

We could barely hear his words, but it didn't matter. Each of us knew this speech by heart. He recited it every year and we never tired of the melodrama.

"Let's take a moment…raise our glasses…and make a solemn pledge. A vow to spend the next four weeks enriching…giving with open hearts…*to each other*." He screamed the last words, pushing us into a frenzy of familial love.

Then, as quickly as we had been roused, we fell into an upbeat hum. The women chatted among themselves about the latest celebrity couples and the men compared rationales for the Redskins's unexpected Super Bowl win over the Dolphins. Dannie and I traded our best *Star Wars* impersonations and quoted movie lines so funny drinks leaked from our noses.

Mikey ran to the table. "Mommy, can you get me some dinner?"

I rolled my eyes. "Go get it yourself. We're eating."

"But I want Mommy to do it." He slumped over and a whine crept into his voice. A full-blown meltdown would follow soon after.

"I'll get it, Champ." Dad stood, winking at Mom, and reached for Mikey's hand.

He pulled back sharply. "No. I want *Mommy* to get it!"

Mom stood slowly, kissed Mikey on the forehead, and walked delicately toward the kitchen. I stared at Dad, incredulous.

"Seriously lazy."

"He's just…I don't know. Coping." Dad took a slow sip of wine and turned to Uncle Richard. "That Lebanon bombing was something else, huh?"

Richard sighed. "I wouldn't want to be in Reagan's shoes right now."

Those at the table nodded and expressed their fears, theories, and predictions quietly. When Mom returned, she continued to pick at her salad. "What are we talking about?"

"The Embassy bombing." I said, my mouth full of spaghetti.

Richard's eyebrows rose. "I'm impressed. Looks like you've been paying attention to the papers?"

"Nah. It's just been on TV all the time."

"Any way you can find to stay current with world events is good with me." Richard chuckled. He was a highly respected New York physician whose calm and soothing demeanor perfectly balanced Tammy's loud and boisterous personality.

Ron threw back his last gulp of whisky and leaned forward, both arms long on the table. He eyed us like co-conspirators.

"What we should do is send in a team. Like The A-Team. Go bomb the fuck out of those bastards. Give them a dose of their own medicine. A little Mr. T action."

"Ron." Patty hissed under her breath. Richard cleared his throat.

Tammy refilled Dad's wine glass. "Want any?" Tammy asked Mom with a slight edge.

"Yes, I should probably have a titch." Mom looked at Tammy as they stifled a laugh.

Everyone ate a few more bites, filling the awkward silence until Dad jumped in. "Richard, I understand you've been up to some pretty amazing things." The relief was palpable.

"Yes. That is, if you find embryos amazing." My parents laughed good-naturedly as Ron pushed back his chair.

"Gross. I need another drink." Ron swayed slightly to the side. Patty gave Tammy an exasperated look.

Tammy pushed the pitcher of water to Ron. "Here, how about some of this?"

"How about some of *this?*" Ron grabbed the wine bottle and emptied its contents into his whisky tumbler.

Richard continued. "I just returned from the UCLA Medical Center." He inhaled slowly. "I'm truly excited about this and, frankly, I get a little superstitious every time I talk about it. I don't want to jinx the project."

Mom laughed. "Jinx it? Well, that's new. A superstitious doctor."

"I swear," Tammy said, "he'd start chanting witch doctor spells if it would ensure this all turns out well." She pressed her lips to Richard's cheek.

Richard leaned forward, his face flushed. "The embryo transfer was successful. If all goes well…and that's a big if"—he leaned in more—"we will have the first human born through artificial insemination of a frozen embryo."

My father shook his head in astonishment. "That's absolutely amazing. I had no idea it was such a large breakthrough. The papers just touched on *happenings* at UCLA but—"

"Speaking of which," Ron jumped in, letting out a small belch, "I notice you didn't visit us while you were out our way." He smiled mischievously, but there was a dangerous twinge in his eyes. Patty slipped her hand under the tablecloth to find Dannie's and interlaced their fingers. Dannie stared vacantly at her plate.

Richard leaned back. "I'm sorry about that, Ron. The trip was definitely business, not pleasure."

"Still, you should have called. I don't remember getting a call. Do you?" Patty ignored Ron's heavy breath at her ear. "Sure would have been the respectful thing to call on your family when you're in the neighborhood. That's what you would do. Out of respect."

The table sat silent as fingers of electric energy jumped and pinched every single one of us. Even so, we remained still until Dad, as family psychologist, smiled softly at Ron and nodded in agreement. "Yes, that would have been the respectful thing to do. I'm sure Richard feels terrible he didn't call."

The half-second look that passed between Dad and Richard contained a whole conversation: Dad told Richard that Ron was teetering on the edge; no one agreed with his boorish behavior; no one appreciated his presence in the family anymore; and that Dad and Richard, as educated and ethical leaders of our family, needed to rise above Ron's neanderthal mentality to ensure a peaceful remainder of the dinner.

Richard turned to Ron, remorse in his eyes. "I do feel terrible, Ron. I should have called. Won't be making that mistake again."

Ron nodded and took another gulp of wine. He stared at the glass for a moment, then bared his teeth, his smile frighteningly animated. "Hey! It's ok, right? We're family."

Tammy sat back hard, holding in a thundercloud of words, muttering only, "Oh, please."

Dannie pulled her hand back from Patty and scraped her chair away from the table. "I'm getting more salad." I tried to catch her eye, but she bolted from the room too quickly.

Ron continued, oblivious to the tension he had caused. "Speaking of family, I want to talk to you guys about something I've been developing."

"Developing?" Dad couldn't contain his suspicious tone.

"An idea. A business idea."

The air visibly left the table as the adults, in unison, inhaled sharply and leaned away.

Ron waited. When nobody expressed interest, he plowed ahead.

"Richard, you like golf?"

"Um, yes, I do."

"Jim? You?"

"Occasionally, yes."

"And it's expensive right?" No one responded. "Well, before you spend the big bucks, wouldn't it be nice to know if the course is worth playing?"

The table sat silent.

"My plan is to do the work before you spend the money."

Tammy's brow furrowed. "I don't understand what your *business plan* is."

Ron gave an exasperated look. "I'll go play courses and rate them. Then you can contact me, and for a fee, I'll connect you with the course that's right for you. In your price range, where you'll be staying if it's a vacation, that kind of thing."

"So, basically, you want to golf," Mom said.

"Right, right. But I'll be working. I'll be rating everything. The courses, the services, the club restaurants. And there's more." Ron bounced in his seat with excitement. "The way I see it, executive types play all the time and would want to contact me. You know, a lot of rich guys. They'll see what a great idea I have. Then it's only a matter of time before they put me in touch with someone who works in TV. I think it'll make a great show. I would play a course every episode and rate it right on the air. I'm telling you, it's a sure thing."

Richard crossed his arms over his chest. "Playing these courses, paying for meals, travel to get there…it sounds quite expensive just to do your research. Have you saved the start-up money?"

Patty sat stick still and closed her eyes.

"*That,* my family, is where *you* come in." Ron's eyes glistened in his alcohol-induced, hyper-manic state.

The adults simultaneously pushed away their dinner plates. Some coughed awkwardly as Tammy pushed back from the table, ready to leave.

Dad jumped in. "Ron, it sounds like you're excited about this plan. But it's our first night here. As family, not as business partners."

"But the return you could make—"

Richard bent forward and gave Ron a steely look. "I believe it's time for you to retire for the evening."

Ron looked from person to person, not quite comprehending.

I sat silent, a small mouse. If I remained very still, I might be invisible to the passing, hungry cat.

As I glanced around for Dannie, I caught Amy's eye as she moved toward our table with little Tommy in tow, a bubbly smile sweeping over her face.

"Well, hello Adam. Hello, Mr. Craig." Flushing, Dad nodded. Mom smirked.

The sound of Amy's voice lifted the feeling of doom that had settled deep in my chest. So did the sight of her smile.

"Great dinner," Amy said. "Thank you guys so much. It really was rad."

Tammy smiled. "Why, thank you. And you're very welcome."

"Want to come to the bonfire tonight?" I blurted out and snuck a quick glance at the others. I was relieved to see it hadn't registered any reactions. Expectantly, I turned back to Amy, an image flashing in my mind: Amy and I, warmed by the fire, sharing a single log stool, our thighs pressed together, my arms wrapped tightly around her torso, my face nestled in her hair.

"I'd love to. Really. But"—she tilted her head to Tommy—"Bedtime."

My heart sank.

"But maybe some other night soon?"

"Yeah, okay."

"Great. See you in the morning." As she walked off with Tommy, Amy winked.

A spasm of desire rippled through me.

Ron, who had been scrutinizing Amy closely, turned to the table. "Damn. Now *that's* what I'm talking about." The men looked off, disregarding his comment.

Mom exhaled with disgust as Tammy reached for Patty's hand. She was too late. Patty was already walking away in stoic silence.

I looked back and found Dannie, who had been standing right behind us, watching the whole scene.

⁋

THE BONFIRE WAS packed, as expected. The crowd moved, amoeba-like, from the dining hall to the back lawn, reeling from familial love and a happy, heady wine buzz. Log benches and stools encircled a monstrous fire. Aunts, uncles, cousins old and young sat on laps, on benches, on the ground, arms and bodies tangled, swaying, singing, and laughing.

My cousin Mark strummed his guitar, leading us in a boisterous, ruckus-filled, completely off-key version of *Show Me The Way To Go Home*. We erupted in laughter, then cheered him as he unexpectedly broke into the theme song from *Jaws*. I sat on a bench next to Tammy. Directly across from us, Mom rested her head on Dad's shoulder while Mikey melted into her lap, desperately trying to stay awake.

Dannie approached from behind. Silently, and without looking at me, she slipped in front at my feet, nestling herself between my legs. She laid her head on my lap as I wrapped my arms around her and hugged. All at once, I realized how much I had missed my best friend, the person I could be with, no words spoken and no explanation ever given. Sitting with Dannie, feeling the heat from her back while her muscles relaxed against me, felt like home. Glancing down, Tammy gave me a sad smile and gently kissed my cheek.

A good-natured war had begun between The Feathers and The Means, each demanding that Mark play one of their songs. "Some Go-Go's, Ravyns or at least Tommy Tutone," they screamed.

"Are you kidding me?" Mark bellowed. "That's not even music."

The boys booed him but smiled despite themselves. And as Mark began to play a haunting version of Pink Floyd's *Wish You Were Here*, our clan quieted. We started to sway in rhythm to his voice as it rose over the fire.

I inhaled slowly, deeply, ingesting the smoky air while looking around the circle. The intense heat from the fire made the scene quiver, unearthly and dreamlike. My mother smiled, eyes closed, her fingers entwined with my father's. Tammy leaned into Richard, swaying as she whispered in his ear, making them chuckle softly. I couldn't tell where one cousin began and another ended, they were pressed so closely against each another. My aunts and uncles held their small children close, rocking them softly, keeping them with the family rather than sending them to bed as though it were an initiation. My older cousins hugged each other tightly, relishing these fleeting, carefree days before facing college classes, midterm exams, apprenticeships, and the harsh, real world.

For a second, my mind-trick kicked in again. The love emanating from my family was real. True. A blanket keeping us safe. And right then, for just a moment, I thought we could stay like that forever. But then I looked down at

Dannie. She was singing along with Mark, barely audible, her lips almost unmoving.

Quiet tears streamed down her face.

Chapter 6

"**I** got it!"

Kevin ran forward to pop the volleyball upward, a perfect set. Dannie came down hard and spiked it into the sand on the other side of the net. A collective groan rose from my team as we wiped droplets of sweat from our faces.

I had greatly underestimated Kevin's ability. Dannie and I had reviewed the rosters meticulously, dividing the athletic and older family members evenly between the teams. We separated ourselves as well. Unfortunately, I assumed Kevin would still be one of the little kids, a group we also divided evenly, reminiscing and laughing about our last tournament when the little ones spent more time picking dandelions than touching the ball. In the last two years, though, Kevin had developed physically and honed his skills. Suddenly, not having him on my team put us at a disadvantage.

Dannie high-fived Kevin while the rest of the cousins whooped and yelled disparaging comments in our direction. I called for a huddle.

"This is bad." I said, shaking my head. We only had two more weeks of practice before the big tournament and I resigned myself to the fact that the Mega Monster Trophy, a gaudy bowling prize someone bought at a garage sale years ago, would end up in Dannie's possession at the end of the summer.

"What do you want us to do, Captain?" Eric asked, smacking me lightly on the back. The older cousins loved to pass the torch of team captain onto shoulders other than their own, happy to defer rather than take the responsibility of leadership themselves.

"The best thing we can do is keep the ball out of Dannie's and Kevin's area."

"No shit," Angie said. "Let's just play." She backed away from the huddle. "I'm about to die of heat stroke and a cold beer may be the only thing that'll save me." Sounds of happy agreement rose from the team.

It was pointless to rally my troops. Still, I didn't want to look like I'd lost command, so I yelled again. "Remember, don't hit it *directly* to Dannie or Kev!"

Dannie smirked, then began to cheer mockingly. "We got power, yes we do. Who will win? It won't be you!" She jumped and tried to touch her toes, then pumped imaginary pom-poms in the air as she pranced in a circle.

"Way to kick a man while he's down," I shouted back.

"Aw, poor baby. Don't worry. I'll only keep kicking you until we win. Like, totally. For sure." We pretended to glare at each other until our laughter erupted simultaneously.

Dannie's team served and the volley began. The intensity increased as the ball traveled back and forth over the net.

"Got it."

"I got it!"

"You take it."

"Set it up. You. You!"

"Got it!"

For a moment, it looked like we would win the point as my team kept the ball from Dannie and Kevin. Then, one of the younger Means unexpectedly brought his focus back to the game. Running forward, he hit the ball a foot and a half in the air. Eric dove for the save, sinking deep into the sand as he lobbed the ball high over the net. The ball hovered, then seemed to pause in mid-air directly in front of Dannie. Like an attacking shark, she spiked it straight into Eric's unprotected face as he lay on the ground.

We heard the snap of cartilage and saw blood start to drain down Eric's shirt. Angie took one look and immediately passed out, groaning as she went down. The rest of us rushed to Eric. Fearing he might drown in the river of his own blood, I tilted his face, one hand on each cheek, until the stream ran away from his mouth.

"Oh, God!" Dannie gasped, hyperventilating, "I'm so sorry! Oh God, Eric, oh God, I didn't mean to."

Eric smiled. "No worries babe-a-licious." He winced and pinched his nose tighter, trying to stop the blood that trickled inside his hand and down his wrist. Another Feather took off his T-shirt and handed it to Eric. "Man, that smarts."

Cousin Katie cringed. "Your face is turning purple. I'm getting Richard."

I turned to Dannie. "Hey, it's okay. You didn't mean to."

"Yeah, I'm totally fine," Eric said through a slight gurgle.

Dannie, teary-eyed and incredulous, insisted. "You are *not* fine."

"I may need to sit out of the tourney—"

"You think?" Angie, finally awake, yelled from a safe distance while still laying in the sand.

"—but all in all, I'm fine. Really, sweets, I'm all good."

Katie wrapped her arms around Dannie, squeezing her reassuringly as Richard appeared from around the corner, a ham sandwich in hand. He bent down over Eric, puzzled.

"What's shakin' bacon?"

"Bad choice of words," Eric managed as the group groaned.

Richard pulled the bloody shirt from Eric's face and gently probed his tender nose.

"Well, it's definitely broken."

"Oh, God."

"But we can't do much until the swelling goes down, so it's ice and ibuprofen for you, my friend."

"And beer," Angie chimed in.

Dannie bent down, gently resting her arm on Eric's chest. "I'm sorry. Really."

"Babe, I'm a guy. We look rad with broken noses." He smiled at Dannie and playfully tousled her hair.

Terry stood and stretched his large arms, helping Eric to his feet. "Time to adjourn to the keg for the day." The rest of the group whooped in agreement as they huddled around Eric and walked together to the beach. The younger players had already meandered off, leaving Dannie and I deserted on the volleyball court, surrounded only by red sand.

"Wow," I said. "You really will do anything to win, huh?"

Dannie turned and darted away.

"I'm kidding. Wait up, I'm just kidding." I ran as she marched into the lodge, grabbing her shoulders from behind when I caught up, squeezing tight. "Come on. I was just joshin'."

"It's not funny. I really hurt him, and I feel shitty."

"You didn't mean to."

"I know, but I still feel terrible. And now you're a player short."

"Yeah." I stopped to consider the loss. Kevin had been a surprise, but I doubted there was another ringer in the family. "I guess we're screwed."

"I don't know if nonfamily can play, but I'm not half bad."

We turned to find Amy sprawled on the side porch, playing Jacks with Tommy. I internally gasped as I took her in. Short-short cutoff jeans that showcased her oiled, glistening legs. A hot pink mesh tank top clinging tight over a string bikini thin as dental floss. Her mass of glossy hair piled high on her head. She smiled at me with cherry-glossed lips, her tanned face glowing.

Once again, I was entranced.

"Yeah, I don't think we allow babysitters," Dannie said curtly.

I snapped to attention. "Says who? It's never come up before. Let's take a vote. I vote yes." I smiled my most beguiling smile. Amy winked and my knees nearly buckled.

I looked at Dannie, who looked at me, then at Amy.

"Well?" Amy asked, her eyes on Dannie.

Begrudgingly, Dannie turned back to me and sighed. "Since I got us in this mess, and I don't want to be an asshole for a second time today, I guess I vote yes, too."

Amy smiled at her. "Bitchin'."

To my surprise, Dannie smiled back.

"Bitchin'."

Chapter 7

I was in our living room in Chicago. My stuffed animals, every one of them decimated and destroyed, were strewn around the floor and covered the furniture. Shaggy-maned lion heads were torn from their bodies, teddy bear carcasses lay limp and dismembered on the couch. Stuffing floated through the air, a macabre snowfall.

Behind me, the sharp, tinny rendition of a carnival theme song began to play, threatening and menacing. Kevin, then Mikey, then Dad darted in and out of the room, giggling as they rounded corners into the honeycomb of hallways. I was afraid and called out for them to stop, but they only sped up their animated chase, ignoring me while racing through the wallpapered maze. I cursed my lethargic feet, unable to push my body forward with the overwhelming sense of urgency I felt as I tried desperately to reach them.

Then I was falling backward off our front balcony. Only it wasn't our house, and it wasn't our balcony. The act of falling took my breath away and I squeezed my eyes shut. I hit the ground but felt no pain. Before I knew it, I was running to the balcony, beginning the process all over again. I was calling out for help, for someone to catch me, to hold me back as I jumped, sprawled flat like a kite, my face to the sky. No sound came from my throat as I cried out in vain. Again I landed, and again I ran. I attempted to scream, falling victim to confusion and fear. It overwhelmed my body as my breath came only in deep spasms.

Then my mother was holding me. I was wrapped tight in my favorite childhood blanket, swaddled like a baby. She sang to me, serenely rocking my body. Her warm hand was on my face, her eyes inches from my own, singing tenderly, calming me…

৯

MY EYES FINALLY forced themselves open. I was still half-present in the deep nightmare, my face and pillow soaked with real tears that flowed with fear and panic.

Mom folded me in her arms and stroked my cheek while whispering in my ear. "Shhhh, my love. Shhhh. Wake up. It's only a dream. Shhhh, my love." She smiled gently at my confusion and cradled my head into her lap as she chased the demons from my mind.

"Poor thing. Must have been a heck of a game today, huh? You've been out cold for a couple of hours. I didn't want you to have a hard time sleeping tonight, so I thought I'd wake you up." She stroked my hair and smiled again. "I'm glad I came in when I did. You were having a doozie of a bad dream."

I stayed on her lap and took in the thick pine wood scent, the dense orange afternoon light, and the security of my mother's hand. I nestled my head deeper into her body and succumbed to her soft humming. I closed my eyes and felt the well-worn yarn of her cardigan. The scent of her flowery soap and familiar hand lotion filled my nostrils as I tried to breath normally, pushing away my very real fear of falling again.

Chapter 8

The beach buzzed with the smallest Minnows and a gaggle of aunts, who chirped cautions and reprimands from their plastic folding lounge chairs while retelling old family stories and sending each other into fits of laughter. Pitchers of vodka lemonade were passed around and the ice in their large plastic cups cracked and popped on contact.

"Send that over here. We need refills," Tammy shouted over the shrieks and hysteria while a large pitcher went down the line. The chairs were placed in a large circle with wicker ottomans scattered in between, holding beverages and bowls of pretzels and chips. Mom smiled at the scene, sitting in the cool shade under an enormous, overbearing pine tree. Next to her, Patty sipped her vodka, throwing off carefree laughs.

My aunt Ann continued her story of a large family ski trip when the women were still teenagers. "Remember when Grannie and Gennie and all of our moms were three sheets to the wind from après-ski? And poor Tammy was laying there with a broken ankle!"

"Not my fault. Those skis were so shitty then, weren't they?" Tammy held her head high in mock defense. The group broke out in unified protest against the horrid conditions of their old snow gear and railed about the injuries they caused.

"It's unfair how much easier the kids have it today."

"They have no concept of how to really ski."

"These new skis do all the work for you."

"If we'd only had those!"

"Remember that time Carla hurt her knee? Like someone twisting a lemon rind." Groans rose from the group.

"*Anyway*," Ann continued, "while the parents were elbow deep in their martinis and G & T's, we were baked beyond all reason." Another cheer erupted from the women, celebrating their youthful delinquency.

"On top of the weed Chuck brought in."

"Who's Chuck?" Maureen asked and the women jumped in again, shouting amiably.

"I remember Chuck."

"Oh my God, I totally forgot!"

"That guy Kate picked up at the ski lodge."

"Wasn't he like fifty years old?"

"Twenty-five, I think."

"Yeah, but when you're sixteen, twenty-five might as well be fifty."

"Didn't he have a mustache?"

"Yes!"

"He looked just like Burt Reynolds."

More deep belly laughs.

"No way I picked up a Burt Reynolds guy," Kate protested, snorting vodka out of her nose.

"You did, you did!" Tammy screeched, poking her in the arm.

"And remember he brought in the case of beer and Gramps said, *Ok, we're on vacation. You kids can have it—but only that one case*. We kept the case on the coffee table and kept sneaking individual cans in all night in our coats. It was the bottomless case of beer."

Mom groaned. "Oh, I remember that. Sort of." The women all laughed again.

Pauline chuckled and shook her head. "It's amazing we remember any of that night."

"The beer was nothing compared to how much pot we smoked that trip."

Another collective groan.

Beth took another big gulp of vodka. "I'm pretty sure I ended up making out with Ben that night." She was referring to my uncle Ben, her second cousin.

Laughter of volcanic proportion exploded from the group.

"Gross!"

"Stop, please!"

"Too much."

"I didn't know what I was doing. I was tweaked out on hash and ten beers." Beth shrugged her shoulders apathetically.

"The family that makes out together stays together," Jenny chimed in, doubled over in laughter.

Tammy stood, swayed slightly, and raised her glass, "Here's to Burt Reynolds!"

The women all raised their glasses in unison. "To Burt Reynolds!"

The chatter continued and I curled into my lounge chair, a light blanket lying over me. The dream had drained my energy. I languidly scanned the beach. Kids jumped off the shallow end of the dock as they played Sharks and Minnows. The Means used one of the fishing boats as the safety base for King of the Mountain, unaware of the hidden dangers of jagged protruding rocks and razor-sharp propellers.

My eyes rested on a lone figure at the end of the long pier, lean legs dangling over the edge. I squinted and could make out Dannie's long blonde hair. She sat in complete stillness except for the rhythmic sway of her legs, one at a time, forward and back, while she stared straight ahead at the lake.

I followed her feet, hypnotized, lost in my thoughts until a roar of catcalls and whistles came from the aunts. Dad had waltzed out with two fresh pitchers of vodka lemonade and bowed deeply in front of the women. "For the ladies."

Tammy sprang to her feet, grabbed one of the pitchers, and began to fill her neighboring glasses while Dad did the same on the other side of the circle. I watched as he came to a stop in front of Mom. They locked eyes and gazed at each other, oblivious to anyone else. Dad slowly reached his hand out to her face and cupped her chin, transmitting a silent, private message only she could understand. Her eyes closed and for a moment as she rested the full weight of her head in his hand.

In that instant, in the midst of their mutual loving gestures, rage passed through me. My throat tightened and my body tensed. Why was everyone acting like nothing was wrong? Why did we have to pretend everything was normal? Pretend that we weren't scared and frightened and lost in the knowledge that nothing in this world was fair? That nothing would last? My mind seethed thinking of the lost time with my mother. Time I would not have with her in the future and time lost in the ignorance of the past. Why had Mom and Dad wasted so much time bickering about finances, about vacation dates, about who was going to drive me to soccer practice? Why had so much time been wasted grading papers, meeting with students, gossiping with friends on the phone? Why did they argue over who had forgotten to do the dishes or take out the trash? And why now, during the worst, did they act like nothing was wrong? They acted like they were thankful. For what? She was dying, so why did he stroll around filling cocktail glasses and caressing her face as if that could make things better? We needed someone to heal my mother, to fix our future, to secure our family. Not someone who acted like the world was his oyster.

Knocking over my chair, I walked heatedly toward Dannie. My steps echoed and rattled, and the rickety pier shook to-and-fro under me as my feet hit the weathered wood. Dannie didn't look up as I fell in next to her with a thud. I could see her shoulders shaking softly and I glanced at her streaked face. She showed no emotion. No sorrow. No anger. The only cracks visible in her armor were the tears dripping off her chin. I looked out at the lake as the sun began its evening descent.

"My parents are getting a divorce." Her words were barely audible.

I nodded, silently, keeping my focus on the lake.

"My mom is dying."

And with that phrase, every molecule of anger fell away, leaving me exhausted. I felt my own tears begin, velvet ribbons tracing my cheeks, chin, and neck. Dannie remained wordless, but her hand reached out and found mine. We held onto each other in silence and cried as we contemplated what had once been a place of innocent bonding.

Black Bear Lake would never be that again.

The sun lowered and the dinner bell rang. Neither of us moved. As the sun set, we heard families moving slowly out of the dining hall with full bellies. They migrated towards their cabins with titters and guffaw-filled conversation while simultaneously shouting out bedtime commands.

Dannie softly tugged on my hand. We rolled onto our backs, situating ourselves on the pier and watching stars twinkle in the crystal-clear sky like a vast network of Christmas lights.

Mom and Dad stepped onto the pier behind us.

We didn't move.

"Go tell Adam to come in, will you?" Mom whispered.

Dad paused. "Why don't we let them sleep?"

"We can't let them sleep outside."

"Why not? Remember when we used to camp out under the stars?"

Mom sighed and I could hear amusement in her voice. "I guess one night will be fine."

They walked on while we continued to watch the stars in silence. At some point, Dannie fell asleep, her breath hot on my shoulder. And as I stared at the vast sky, feeling more protected in Dannie's hand than I had in a very long time, I could hear the deep, serene grunts of Old Papa lumbering to the kitchen's back door.

Chapter 9

Dew permeated my clothes until they gripped my body like a cold, wet, blanket. The dock had turned concrete on my back and my hipbone protested loudly where I had been sleeping. The birds were playful in the crisp morning light and loons cried their long, sad song across the lake. I stretched out and breathed in the woodsy air, noticing through closed eyelids a strange shadow moving over me.

I opened my eyes and screamed.

Tommy hovered inches above my face, staring at me, eyes blazing with excitement, a grin stretching from ear to ear.

"It's Nature Arts Day," he whispered directly into my nose.

Nature Arts Day was, without question, our favorite activity at Black Bear Lake. The day consisted of stomping around in the woods unattended, thrusting hands deep into the sandy soil, making swords out of tree branches and flinging spiders at the babysitters. Nature Arts was Gramps's brainchild and had been going on since before I was born. I found myself giddy thinking of the day ahead.

"Nature Arts Day!" Tommy whispered again, the end trailing off into a shriek as he started jumping up and down, his little naked body, in all its glory, jerking spastically from side to side.

I threw my hand up over my face. "Okay, okay, let me have some breakfast first." I pulled myself to my knees to see Amy and Dannie doubled over in laughter at the sight of Tommy violently shaking all his parts directly at my face.

∽

"GODDAMMIT," GRAMPS BELLOWED from the breakfast table in the kitchen. "I don't want goddamn fish and bagels. I want bacon and pancakes."

Tammy took a large bite out of hers, unfazed. "It's called lox and bagels, Daddy, and I brought them fresh all the way from New York. They're delicious. Try some." Tammy held out her other half and Gramps turned away with a huff, causing Tammy to shake her head and laugh. "All the more for me."

"Goddammit, Rose, make me some bacon!"

Grannie pulled two bagel halves out of the toaster and put them on a plate, shoved it to the side and put two more halves into the toaster. Although it was a breakfast anyone with half a brain could fix himself, Grannie felt the need to set up a cooking assembly line and oversee her operation.

"For goodness' sake, Charles. Quit yelling. Have a bagel."

Gramps eyes grew big. "I don't want a bagel. Didn't I just say that? Now throw some bacon on before it turns from breakfast to lunch time."

"You'll have a bagel, or you'll have some cold cereal. I'm not making bacon or pancakes this morning."

"Or eggs," Aunt Gennie chimed in. "The gas is out again."

Grannie gave Genevieve a stern look. "I told you not to say anything," she whispered harshly.

Gramps's face turned four shades darker. He shot out of his chair, chest puffed with adrenaline. "And the gas company has the goddamn nerve to tell me there's nothing wrong."

The kitchen table was elbow-deep in cream cheese-filled smirks as we desperately tried to stifle our laughter.

"Daddy, don't run off yet. You have to kick off Nature Arts." Tammy winked at me as we threw knowing looks at each other. Gramps couldn't pass up his moment in the spotlight, and Tammy's words stopped him in his tracks.

"Well, dammit then, get the kids together," he yelled before thundering out the back door toward the beach.

"Maybe you kids can take him into the woods with you today," Grannie said with a gleam in her eye.

"Not a chance." I laughed and grabbed the second half of my bagel. "Come on guys." Dannie, Amy, and I headed out after Gramps with Tommy leading the way, skipping happily.

The beach was filled with twenty-seven kids and a collection of babysitters, all antsy and anxious with bubbling energy. Gramps beamed at the sight of his minions as they ran, toppling and tumbling over each other like a pack of lion cubs.

"Ok, quiet…quiet…QUIET!" The pandemonium mellowed to reasonable mayhem as the kids tried their hardest, yet failed, to focus their attention.

Gramps went on. "Nature Arts Day!"

The group exploded in cheers and shouts.

"Group up with whomever you like. You have four hours from now to return with your nature loot. You must be back by"—Gramps checked his watch in mock seriousness—"noon. OR…you will be disqualified."

The kids were to gather anything that inspired them, grabbed their attention, or made them think of Black Bear Lake. They would then reconvene on the beach. Their collected items surrounding them, each would write a poem on what the lake and our family meant to them. They would then take the poem and woodsy items and create a collage for Gramps. He would go through the projects, one by one, dismissing them as he went until deciding on the project he liked best.

The artwork chosen always gave Gramps the most adoration and praise. Every year, the mothers protested that his favoritism would damage the children's' psyches, yet Nature Arts Day proceeded without fail. Truth was, we all loved scavenging through the underbrush and the exhilarating freedom that came with our exploration. For one day, we were adventurers, archeologists, and crash survivors lost in a jungle. The contest was furthest from our minds.

The Minnows bubbled with excitement, like bird dogs waiting for the command to fetch.

"Now get going!"

The group burst apart as kids ran for the woods. The babysitters trailed behind with little concern, chatting about which Feather they were crushing on.

Mikey came running to Tommy. "Let's go together!" Tommy sprang up and down again; the excitement reached such frenzy he had lost his power of speech. He grabbed Mikey's hand and they dashed off towards the tree line.

Dannie, Amy, and I meandered behind them.

Dannie raised her eyebrows in surprise. "Mikey's really into Tommy this year."

"I know. It's strange." As we entered the woods, I absently picked a leaf from a branch, pulling it low and letting it snap back hard. "But at least it's keeping him busy."

"Sometimes I wish I had a little brother or sister." Amy reached high to pull at a branch. Her top, cropped at her midriff, rose with her arm. She wasn't wearing a bra. I breathed in quick and tried to silence my racing heart. Amy glanced at me, and my face burned despite the shade that had swallowed us. She smirked.

"Me, too," Dannie said. "It would be nice for my parents to focus on someone else."

"I wonder which is worse," Amy said to the sky, "to have parents that focus on you or have parents that don't care." She paused. "At all."

None of us answered, lost in the thoughts of our current situations.

We walked in silence, pulling at tall blades of grass and low-hanging leaves. Softly, Dannie began to hum. Amy smiled. "Sing louder. So we can hear you."

Dannie sang a slow, sad rendition of Neil Young's *Helpless* as we strolled through the woods. My mind swirled and was vacant all at once. My heart ached at their words because for the first time, clear as glass, I could see how good my life was. How complete my family was. My mind wasn't tricking me. Mom and Dad cared desperately about us, and I was lucky. I had something special. But it was going away, vanishing like a ghost. Our time together was finite.

Just as that familiar lump of despair began to form in my throat, Amy let out a whistle. "Whoa."

Dannie stopped singing as we stood in awe.

Ahead of us was the largest clearing I had never seen. Sunbeams shone on a large circle of lime-green grass like something out of a fairy tale. We smiled and ran for our secret garden. I hit the spot first and did a somersault, landing spread eagle, the warm rays penetrating my lost thoughts of despair. Amy and Dannie followed, and we all lay flat on our backs, joy stretched wide across our faces, eyes closed to the sunlight covering us like a blanket.

Eventually, out of her pocket Amy pulled out a soft pack of Marlboro Lights and lit one. Blowing a stream of silky smoke into the air, she rolled over onto her side. "You have a beautiful voice."

"She always has. *She sings mah-va-lous!*" I mocked.

Dannie grinned and threw a pine cone at my head.

"Do you sing a lot? I mean, at school or something? Like in a choir?"

Dannie propped herself up against a tree stump and began picking blades of grass. "Nah. Just for myself. And with numb-nuts over there."

"You sing?" Amy turned with surprise.

It was my turn to throw a pinecone at Dannie's head, with a little extra force behind it. "No. I don't sing at all."

"He writes songs."

"I write poetry, not songs." As soon as the words came out of my mouth, I regretted them. I had instantly shaped Amy's image of me. No longer was I a sporty, carefree, fun-loving everyman. I was immediately thrust into the role of the quiet, nerdy wallflower who sat on the sidelines, emaciated and pale, hunched over his notebook. I kept my eyes on a beetle making its long journey through a pile of wet leaves.

"Yeah, and I sing them" Dannie said, beaming at me. She was herself and never felt the need to apologize—

something I had always loved about her and found comfort in. She could sing, and she would sing to the world. She would sing loud when requested, without censorship, and she showcased me in the same way.

I snuck a peek at Amy just as she blew out a cloud of cigarette smoke. She didn't look at me with cynical amusement or disdain. She looked at me with something I hadn't experienced before. With Tessa, it was teenage lustfulness. But Amy was peering deep into my soul with interest, her eyes layered with intrigue I couldn't comprehend. Then she gave me that sideways smirk and turned to Dannie.

"You should totally come out to Chicago sometime and sing at one of the bars."

Dannie rolled her eyes. "Like we don't have venues in LA?"

"Yeah, but it's all about being connected. I could get you hooked up at who knows how many places."

"What? Like the booking guys know you?" Dannie cocked her head as she challenged Amy's claim.

"Booking agents. Bands. Bartenders. Bouncers. Whoever. They know me."

"Because of your dad?" I had a vision of Amy working in her dad's restaurant. The two of them heading out after hours, tired and covered in spilled sauces and roulades that the aprons didn't catch. They would walk slowly, passing each bar along the way, tipping their heads hello, knowing everyone by name after a few years of this.

"Nope. I just go whenever I want. They always let me in."

This time Dannie looked at her with sincere curiosity. "How do you get in? Do you have a fake I.D.?"

Amy laughed. "No. Well, I guess, maybe." She cupped her breasts together and lifted them slightly. "If you count these."

Dannie and I covered our eyes and mouths, doubling over laughing. My romantic vision of Amy and her dad vanished. Instead, I pictured Amy wearing a tight mini skirt and tube top, winking at bouncers who didn't hesitate to let her past.

Dannie, still blushing slightly, rolled onto her stomach. "But you don't really sleep with them, do you?"

Amy shrugged. "Not all of them, of course. Just the ones that matter."

My eyes grew wider.

"Who matters?" Dannie asked like an apt pupil.

Amy sighed slightly, letting out a slow stream of smoke before leaning in. "Listen, sexuality is currency. But sex is power."

Dannie and I held our breath while our mouths gaped at Amy's frankness.

She continued. "So, you save it for the people with power."

Dannie kept her eyes locked on Amy, who took a drag from her smoke.

"Do you love them?"

We jumped at Amy's forceful laugh. "Love? Oh man, you have a lot of learning to do." She leaned back on her elbows again, eyes surveying her own body as she ashed the cigarette. "What's love got to do with anything?"

"Well, I think it's a good thing to...I mean, you don't have to wait until you're married, but shouldn't that be what you're really trying to look for and find? Love?"

"How many married couples who supposedly love each other are still together? How many married people, who start out saying, *Oh darling, my love, smoochie smoochie, let's get married and live happily ever after because we looooove each other*, how many are still together? How many still feel that way? Feel love?" Amy gathered speed and sat forward. "And then all this love, all these forever feelings that people *think* they have, where does it actually get them? All those high hopes and dreams. They love each other so much they need to spread that love and show the world how concrete those feelings are through some dense, fleshy manifestation. So, they have kids, bring them into the world, into their bubble of fantasy, all because these crazy pheromones have them feeling like they've smoked some really good weed. And then, what happens? The high wears off. The day-to-day sets in and all those things that made them feel *smoochie smoochie* now make them nauseous, make them want to go for the jugular every time they pass in the hallway. They fight. They fight over everything. What to eat, how much money they're making or not making, how they're squeezing the toothpaste tube. Anything to vent the rage boiling in their gut. The feeling of being trapped with not only a spouse but now kids. Everyone loses."

Dannie's eyes swelled with tears that threatened to drop as Amy's words became more forceful.

"The worst part is that most people are too stupid to walk away with something. In fact, they usually end up in a deeper hole than when they started. Debt. Mortgages. Shitty outlooks on life and low self-esteem. Not to mention, now they have these kids in tow that drain them even further."

"You don't have a very high opinion of kids, do you?" I asked.

"It's not that. It's that as soon as shit hits the fan, the kids stop being kids and start being obstacles keeping parents from doing what they really want." Amy snuffed out the tip of her cigarette and turned to Dannie. "Be honest, how wanted do you feel right now?"

Dannie blanched.

Amy closed her eyes for a moment and took a long breath. "I'm sorry. That was low." She reached over, plucked a handful of grass, and tossed it at Dannie. "I guess I'm just going off my own experience."

Dannie stared at her foot and shook her head. "You're right. My parents are at each other's throats. It's a minefield at home. I never know where to go or what to say because at any moment something might explode."

Amy nodded.

A wave of anger towards Amy rushed over me. For causing Dannie to cry and for ruining Nature Arts Day, our favorite day alone Up North. It was our day to escape, to be children, and she had just destroyed ten years of our innocence. I was angry with her for confusing me and filling me with lust and cravings and insecurities during the one time of year I could thwart the pitfalls of adolescence. All I wanted to do in that moment was run carefree through the woods, across the beach, and into the lake.

"My parents still love each other." I snapped. "They're still happy." In the back of mind, I knew Amy had hit on some truths. Mom and Dad did love each other, and they were happy together. But that time of happiness would not last. An unavoidable end to their love and happiness was bearing down on them, and it occurred to me for the first time how great this loss would be for my father.

Kevin, Mikey, and I were lucky. We were given Mom. We had no choice and by pure chance ended up with her to care for us.

But of the millions of women in the world, Dad *chose* her. He chose the soft-spoken voice, the shining brunette curls, the petal pink lips. He chose her laughter. He chose her gentle nature. He chose her love of flowers, of babies, of all things pure and natural.

Dad had dated and decided whom he wanted to spend the rest of his life with. He had decided on Mom. And they were happy.

So, what would he do after she was gone? My crush on Tessa had only been alive for a few months and I still couldn't stop thinking about her. How was Dad going to manage after almost twenty years of true love?

For the small amount of time I had allowed myself to think about it, I assumed we would just march forward, four men continuing to live. Dad and I would split up chores around the house. He would continue to teach at the university, maybe take on a summer class to make up for Mom's lost income. I would learn to cook more than a PB&J and do the laundry without turning everything pink. I would get my driver's license the next fall, do the grocery shopping and take Mikey and Kevin wherever they needed to go.

We would soldier on.

But what if we didn't? What if Dad became lonely and needed to meet someone? What if he *did* meet someone?

The questions came at machine-gun speed.

Would he leave us at night? Leave me to stay with Mikey and Kevin while he went out to dinners or movies or to her apartment? Would he date a lot of women, or would he immediately find one that filled the void left by Mom's passing?

Could he ever truly fill that empty space? Could he replace her?

What if he did become serious with one woman? Would she be like my mother? Soft, quiet, kind. Or would she be the opposite? Loud, harsh, sharp—everything Mom was not. Would they be content to date the rest of their lives, or would Dad ask this woman to marry him? Would there suddenly be another woman living in our house? Making our beds, feeding us, making sure we had gloves and hats before leaving the house? Or would she not care about us, regard us only as ugly reminders that she was not Dad's first love? Would she resent that we knew she was a stand-in wife? Would she want to start a family of her own with Dad and find a way to distinguish her own family from ours? Would we have to help take care of these new kids? Would we be treated as siblings, or would we be considered the *other* family? Would they become priority? Would we be pushed to the side in favor of these new kids and this new wife?

But what if I liked the new kids?

Or worse yet, what if I liked the new wife?

That thought scared me more than any other. The betrayal of accepting a new woman to replace my mother chilled me. How strange to think I could forget that the new person had not always been there, that her new ways would at a certain point no longer be new, but normal.

At that moment, I knew Amy was right. Love did not last.

"You know, I'm serious when I say you can move in with me while all this shit is going on with your parents," Amy told Dannie, thankfully ignoring my sappy declaration of a loving family.

"I don't know. I mean, it's like, really bad for sure. But still…"

"You said it's a minefield, right? That it's constant fighting?"

"Yeah."

"So, come stay with me. Even just for a semester. They'd probably like it. They wouldn't have to tiptoe around and worry about you on top of all their other problems." Her eyes seemed to search Dannie's face. "Plus, we could hang out with Walt Whitman over here."

Dannie smiled, warming to the idea. "That would be pretty cool."

"I doubt my parents would let me go hang at the Metro." I pictured an embarrassing image of Dannie and Amy free as birds, inviting me to experience whatever adventure awaited in the swirling mix of sex, drugs, and rock 'n roll, only to be sent away by my parents who insisted it was past my bedtime.

Amy laughed. "We could always go to a coffee shop and read poetry, Daddy-O." She purred her words and snapped her fingers rhythmically. I rolled my eyes, acting nonchalant as my face betrayed me, burning red.

"I'm sorry. I was just messing around."

I took a breath and tried to control the shake in my voice. "It's cool."

"Tell me about it." Amy's face was open and inviting.

"About what?"

"How did you start writing? "

I looked to see if she was teasing me again, but she blinked her eyes softly and seemed genuinely interested, though I was learning she was a hard book to read.

"I guess I've liked it since I can remember. My mom used to read to us before bed. Everything except *kid books*." I lifted my hands to make air quotes. "She said if our minds were going to soak up knowledge like a sponge, she wanted us soaking up something valuable. Shakespeare, Keats, Plath, Ginsberg, you name it. She's happiest while reading, so I guess she taught us to like it, too. Anyway, it struck me one night that there are only so many words out there. It's not like they go on indefinitely. So, why is some writing so beautiful, so lyrical and rhythmic like music, and some just puts you to sleep? I started re-arranging words in sentences I'd read to see if I could make them flow better, like water in a stream instead of chunks of concrete. It became a game. I'd lie in the dark, under the covers with a book and flashlight, and go sentence by sentence and see if I could make them sound like music. There's a rhythm to beautiful writing, just like a song. So, I—"

"I want to hear." Amy's sudden intensity made me uncomfortable, and I shifted on the grass.

"Hear what?"

"One of your poems. I want to hear your music. Your water."

I stumbled on my nervousness. "Oh. Well, I don't—"

Dannie jumped in enthusiastically. "This one is my favorite!" She closed her eyes, took a deep breath, and smiled ever so slightly as she began to recite:

The sun could not know
How untruthful it sang,
When beams fell quickly
Creating your halo.

"Come" you said, grabbing my hand.
Our sweaty palms bonded with laughter.
Central Park beckoning, you shout,
"What a journey we will have!"

Under your breath you whisper a language
To a God only you understand.
Some prayer that leaves me lost, afraid, with
Your lips moving in rhythm to invisible dancing demons.

My toes dipped in the cool pond,
Wiggling as minnows nibble, while you
Swam in lazy circles on your back.
Smiling at the heavens, laughing at angels.

I wake to find you naked, shivering.
Standing at the frosted window
As the candle throws monsters who mimic
Your words, "Do you hear them?"

"I cannot get close enough," you said with a grin.
"I want our blood to mix,
Beat together along shared veins. One heart."
I smile, eyes cast down, my hand held too tight.

Trees rush by as blurry serpents.
Rusty leaves throwing shadows as

They flash in the rear-view mirror and
You snap, startled eyes, sized to hold the moon.

A chill runs down my spine.

When she finished, the silence between us roared through my ears. My mixture of embarrassment, anxiety, and self-doubt was lethal, and it took all the strength I had to raise my eyes from my fidgeting fingers.

We sat unmoving, the sun blazing down, and I felt a bead of sweat run down my back.

Amy crawled the few steps to me on her hands and knees and sat squarely in front of me, her stare serious. She cupped my face in her hands and softly kissed me, her eyes still open. I was paralyzed. She pulled back, then kissed me again, and this time I could taste the smoke on her lips. She sank back on her heels and looked at me a beat longer, then stood and raised her arms to the sky, stretching out her cat-like body and smiling serenely.

Dannie's jaw hung open and she looked at me, questioning with eyes wide as saucers. All I could do was shake my head in disbelief and shrug.

Amy's thinking snapped in another direction, and she narrowed her eyes while turning in a full circle, scanning the woods.

"I wonder where the kids ran off to?"

Blood rushed to my face and then drained back out. Dannie's face also went white as we sprang to our feet and running, zigzagging between trees and hurdling stumps.

"Tommy!"

"Mikey! Where are you?!"

"Tommy! Mikey!"

Amy yelled from far behind us, "What's wrong? They're just exploring."

Dannie didn't stop running as she screamed back. "There are bears and wolves out here!" We were both hyperventilating as we ran and shouted.

"Mikey! Mikey!" My voice was quickly going hoarse. Dannie turned to me as she leapt over a mound of sticks and moss. "What if they run into Old Papa?"

"Don't say that! Don't even say that!" I slid on a bed of wet leaves and stumbled over a large log as horrific scenarios sped through my brain. Two small, bloody bodies, shredded by knife-sharp bear claws. Or the half-eaten remains of a wolf pack's easy summer meal. Or two drowned bodies floating just offshore in the lake, not far from where they had wandered in.

I was nauseated. I stopped and turned back to see Amy. She waved her arms in big circles, then motioned for us to be quiet as she continued to beckon excitedly.

"What… did you find…" I yelled between gasps for air. Amy again put her fingers to her lips and shushed me. Dannie and I ran towards her.

As we approached, I saw Mikey not far in the distance.

"Dammit, Mikey! I thought you were dead!" Mikey made the same quiet signal and waved his hand, asking us to follow him. I bent over, put my head between my knees, and let the blood rush back.

On wobbly, adrenaline injected legs, we followed Mikey deeper into the woods. He pointed ahead to Tommy, who was crouched behind a large, rotted tree stump, looking every bit the part of a naked woodland nymph. Tommy waved to us and pointed in front of him.

We gasped.

In the small clearing, lying still and alone, was a newborn fawn. His spotted coat was still wet from the afterbirth. His head bobbed as he gained control of his body.

I looked around but couldn't see the mother. I hoped she was hiding nearby, waiting for us to leave. But after losing Mikey for the short time, morbid images and thoughts continued to swirl in my head and I knew the fawn was permanently alone.

Still, the sheer joy on the faces of my family was infectious, and I found myself similarly enchanted with the beauty of this frail babe. It was the first time I saw something that made me think, *What a miracle*. My heart swelled with love for the delicate and vulnerable creature. I looked around from Amy, whose eyes glistened with tears of happiness and compassion; to Dannie, who glanced at me, a pure and innocent smile on her face, nodding at me in agreement at the beauty; to Mikey, who was gently waving to the fawn as if it would respond; and to Tommy, whose hands cupped over his mouth as he tried to stifle bubbling giggles as best as he could.

Then slowly, on stumbling and unsteady legs, the fawn lifted itself up. It fell two steps to the right, then two to the left before balancing upright.

That's when the sound began.

The fawn cried out once, frail and weak.

The second cry came harder. Desperate. Frantic.

The others were sympathetic with murmurs of "Poor baby" and "Aww". To me, it brought back the panicked feeling of mortality again.

Every bleat cut straight into my body. I could feel the pain and the fear. There was a panic, a hopelessness to each cry, and there was nothing I could do to stop it. I squeezed my eyes shut and tried to block out the noise. But on it went, crying and crying for its mother. I wanted to scream for it to stop, to cover my ears and run. Instead, I stood, barely breathing, ingesting each cry as my own. The desperate cries for a mother.

For a mother who would never return.

Chapter 10

I t had been exceptionally warm, but the next morning saw
90 degrees by 10 a.m. with humidity that wrapped
around us like a wet wool blanket. There was no way to
escape the heat and every activity left us passed out in a pool
of sweat.

The Feathers sat shaded in lounge chairs with buckets of
ice beside them. They rubbed cube after cube over their
temples, stomachs, and hips until they melted. Mom and
Tammy sat inside the lodge in front of an oversized
oscillating fan, playing a silent game of Scrabble, with only
enough energy to lift an eyebrow when a word was in
question. The men sat in the bar as a Cubs game blared from
the television. They held ice-cold beers, more to cool their
hands than to drink. And the Minnows ran around the
grounds completely oblivious to the oppressive heat. We'd
teased Aunt Gennie when we first arrived for ordering a
delivery of Bomb Pops that filled the entire freezer. Now,
there was not a hand that didn't hold a dripping mound of
frozen sugar. She laughed while passing them out at
breakfast, explaining, "We went through a heat wave when
we were younger, and I could tell by the weather this last
April that we'd have the same damn heat again. I told you,
Rose, didn't I?"

"Mmhmm." Grannie nodded while she sucked on her pop
and fanned herself with a newspaper.

"You remember that summer, Charles?"

"Worst goddamn summer I can remember," Gramps harrumphed. "Father got so angry with us for moaning about the heat that he sent us into the forest to cut firewood. Well, all of us except little princess over there." He gestured to Aunt Gennie angrily, his grudge still evident.

Genevieve just winked at the kids and continued to pass out popsicles.

Outside, the Minnows and Means took running jumps off the end of the pier into the lake, burning their feet on the scorching wooden planks. They screeched in painful ecstasy. Tommy and Mikey ran, hand in hand, and launched themselves into the air. Their arms and legs flailed perilously, then smacked hard onto the water's surface.

Dannie, Amy, and I sat on the sandy bottom of the lake, the lukewarm water up to our waists, sucking on Bomb Pops and trying to move as little as possible.

"I think it's sweet how attached at the hip Tommy and Mikey are," Amy said.

I disagreed. "It's a little weird. I mean, with the age difference and everything. When you're eight, you're not supposed to want to hang with a four-year-old." I caught a drip of blue syrup making its way down my popsicle stick and sucked it in.

"It sure has made my job up here easy." Amy paused. "It's got to be nice having so many cousins. You have so much family. It seems...I don't know. Safe."

"Try suffocating." Dannie said as she closed her eyes and turned her face to the sun.

"I wouldn't know." Amy continued to look out at Tommy.

"How many cousins do you have?" I asked.

"None."

Dannie and I looked at each other, lost in the wonder of how life would be if we were not constantly caught in the spider web of family entanglement.

"Jeez, how totally awesome!" Dannie grinned.

"Hey!" I gave her a hurt pout.

She laughed. "Okay. But think about it. Let's just say it was you and me. That's it. We could actually have a private conversation without twenty people asking what we're talking about."

"We could go to dinner without fear of showing up to only wilted salad and pinto beans," I added.

"Or you could sit out back without being asked to babysit for *just a second.*"

"Or being asked to gas up the boats."

"Gather up the towels."

"Clean all the fish the kids caught."

"Wash up the lunch dishes so the moms can sit out back and drink their vodka lemonades."

I smiled. "You win."

Dannie grinned and threw her shoulder against mine. "How about if it *was* just you and me. That would be so rad, wouldn't it?"

"Well, it would be quieter, that's for sure." I smiled. We looked out at Kevin and his group as they yelled out taunts and threats, hurling sand bombs at one another.

"I think it would be awesome if it was the three of us." Amy said quietly. "But really, I'd take any of this." Her toes found mine underwater and she gently stroked them. "Any of it." Blood raced through my body, and I was extremely thankful my lap was hidden under water.

From behind the lodge, the sound of honking horns and motors carried through the air. Everyone looked up and smiled.

It was the Road Rally.

Gramps stored an impressive collection of roadsters and muscle cars at the camp. Once every summer, the men would choose their favorite and race through the backwoods roads, winding their way an hour north up to Duluth, Minnesota. They ended at a seedy bar, where they ate fried cheese curds and drank cold draft beer before leisurely returning to camp. I'd been invited to ride along the last two years and loved it. Usually, one of the Feathers would sneak me a small Solo cup of Leinenkugel and I would cringe with each sip until finishing.

I loved the dirty jokes the bartender would tell and laughed hysterically, though I rarely knew what they meant. I loved that Dad would give me quarters to play the slot machines, and I never got upset despite always losing. I loved being with the group. I loved being a part of the fraternity. I loved returning to camp able to verify the comical stories as the men relived them. I loved how a cousin or uncle or Gramps, or better yet, Dad, would pull up a chair up for me with a smile because we had spent a *Man's Day* together.

But this year, the intense heat had drained all energy and interest from me.

Dad stepped out from the lodge and spotted me. "Road Rally, Adam. Let's go!"

"It's too hot." Just calling out a response fatigued me. "I'm going to skip it."

"Like hell you are!" Gramps's voice boomed out from behind my father. "Come on, I want you to ride with me this year."

I sank underwater, defeated.

Dannie grinned impishly at me. "Sucker."

Amy jabbed Dannie's shoulder with her melting Bomb Pop, wielding it like a sword.

"Hey!" Dannie feigned shock.

Amy leaned over and sucked the sugary syrup off Dannie's shoulder. "Sucker. Get it? Suck…her…?" I left them giggling in the lake and grudgingly grabbed a towel from a lawn chair.

Gramps stood watching me, hands placed firmly on his hips. "Go get your shorts on, boy, and meet me at the Bambino."

I trudged toward the oversized garage, where all the cars had all been driven out and gassed up, the smell of exhaust filling the Northwoods air. The variety of cars was enormous and, even though they had seen them all before, the men hovered, admired, and ooh'd and ahh'd. There were Camaros, Mustangs, Corvettes, Spiders, and Roadsters in different makes and models and colors of the rainbow. Richard picked a '59 MGA Roadster in a deep hunter green. Ron grabbed a black '78 Corvette that always reminded me of the Batmobile. Dad slid into a '53 Cadillac convertible, cream with a buttery tan interior. The other men piled into a dizzying array of polished chrome and leather interiors. We filled twenty-three cars in all.

Gramps stood by his favorite, a mint-condition Fiat Bambino in candy apple red. He wiped down the front bumper with a soft cloth the way a mother bathes her newborn.

"Get in," Gramps said without looking up.

I slid into the front seat as the mix of engine fumes and Turtle Wax filled me with a warm familiarity.

Gramps got in and started his engine. Immediately, like an army waiting for its commander's orders, the engines behind us ignited and revved. Gramps checked his mirrors and slowly pulled the racer forward. The other cars followed the long winding driveway, creating a multicolored, gleaming snake.

We reached the top of the driveway, where the gravel met the street, and Gramps inched the car out until it was securely on the hard asphalt.

Then he put the full weight of his foot on the gas, and we were off, roaring like a pack of frenzied lions.

The trees sped by as the sun burst through the foliage, while the lush greens and yellows created a living watercolor painting. The air streamed by so fast I gasped excitedly for a breath. Despite my initial reservations, I was thrilled to be on the road. As Gramps accelerated, the engine screamed in my ears and the force of his turns threw me against the door. Loud laughs and squeals erupted from somewhere deep inside me. Gramps glanced sideways at me often, each time radiating his own pleasure. I looked behind me at the caravan, a ribbon of colors falling and rising, an occasional arm flying upward, cheering and fist pumping, thrilled at momentarily losing contact with Earth as the cars crested each hill at breakneck speed.

We eventually hit Highway 53, the end of our first leg. We would drive a thirty-minute stretch until we hit the bridge that crossed over into Duluth. We slowed to fifty-five and Gramps sat back with a satisfactory smile on his face.

"How has school been for you? You make good grades?"

"Yes, sir. Pretty good, anyway. I mean, I ended up with three Bs last year and Dad wasn't really happy with that, but it's still better than most of the other kids."

"I'd say. You have a girlfriend?"

"Not a girlfriend exactly. Well, I guess, kind of. I don't know."

"But testing the waters?"

"Definitely." I smirked.

"Good," he bellowed with a wide smile. "I'm glad to hear you're breaking away from your parents. I love them, they are good people, but they shelter you boys too much. You need to be sneaking out, kissing girls, causing trouble. Not cooped up in a college professor's office or a flower shop with your nose in a book all day. When I was your age…how old are you now?"

"Almost fifteen."

"Jesus! At *almost* fifteen all I could think about was girls. I had an A-plus in that class." Gramps laughed loud and hard at himself. "Have a driver's license yet?"

"Soon." The anticipation of freedom was a constant, beautiful buzz in the back of my brain.

"Ah, even better to woo the young ladies with." He winked at me. "What year are you?"

"I'll be a sophomore."

"High school, *almost* fifteen…oh yes, those are the most magical years of a man's life." He smiled serenely and nodded, lost in his secret memories. "Most magical indeed. You must enjoy these years, Adam. Take advantage of them. No matter what. I did, that's for sure. No regrets. And my father was a sonofabitch. A good man, but a strict bastard." He looked forward, frowning for a moment. "I didn't let that stop me. I wanted to try everything, and I did. But those were different times. Even before the war. And Europe herself was different. I was an immigrant, you know." His voice trailed off slightly and he lost himself in thought, as he frequently did at any mention of World War II.

I only nodded. That he thought there was a chance I didn't know every detail of his or Grannie's history amused me. Their stories had been ingrained in all of us since birth, to remind us of where we came from and what we were made of.

❧

IN 1939, WITH little forewarning, Gramps's family quickly gathered blankets and cured bacon and layered their clothing. Survival won out over breaking hearts as they abandoned their beloved animals and farmland. They hustled away, watching their home disappear in the distance, unaware it was the last time they would ever see it. Soon after, just as rumors had promised, the Germans invaded, and with them came the bombs that leveled the family farmhouse. The German invasion into Poland marked the beginning of World War II.

The family made their way to a displaced persons camp, and after he made sure they were safely settled, Gramps slipped off into the night. He met his three childhood friends—Joseph, Henrick, and Aleksander—in an abandoned barn outside of town, fulfilling a pact they had made the moment talk of war had begun to circulate. Other groups of men and boys had the same idea and had formed small militias. And so, together, they began their journey to the secret camp of the Lesni, the Forest Fighters, an anti-German standing army.

During their four years as guerilla fighters, the friends pushed each other to do more for their cause. They depended on the strength of one another for courage in the constant face of death. Together, the young men were invincible as they fought for their country.

In July of 1944, however, their bond was not enough to stave off the inevitable. Henrick and Gramps were ordered to join Operation Ostra Brama, part of Operation Tempest in Vilnius, while Aleksander left to fight in the Warsaw Uprising. Henrick and Gramps fought alongside Soviet troops and in seven short days regained control of Vilnius from the Germans.

It was only when Henrick and Gramps returned to their camp a month they learned of what Aleksander was facing in Warsaw. Without orders and without permission, the two friends left their Home Army, the Armia Krajowa, and rushed to their brother's aid.

Gramps and Henrick used their training to slip into Warsaw, hiding in the rubble and using silent communication to maneuver around posts. After scouring the city for three days, they came upon a captured rebel being marched to the middle of the street. As the soldiers were turned to face the crowd, Henrick gasped quietly. "No, God, no."

Aleksander.

Though badly wounded, he stood tall and unflinching. His eyes scanned the city and fell, without reaction, on his brothers. Gramps and Henrick held eye contact, refusing to look away as they lived Aleksander's final moments with him.

When Poland's AK disbanded in 1945, Gramps made the long journey to join his family in America.

The family, too, had seen much tragedy. Their lives had been changed forever in the DP camp, where they had weathered harsh living conditions for nearly three years. Gramps's youngest brother, Jan, had contracted tuberculosis and finally succumbed to the disease a month shy of the family's relocation to America.

The family arrived in the States and was sent immediately to Chicago, where a large Polish community was already established. Genevieve, barely a teenager, was the only family member with a solid grasp of the English language, putting her firmly in charge of the family's wellbeing. While Genevieve and her brothers went to school, their mother and father found work with fellow immigrants in the Chicago stockyards. The days were grueling and the pay little, but the experience paved the way for a better life.

By the time Gramps reached his family, his father had learned second-hand how the mechanics of refrigerators worked and how to fix them. He had also learned enough broken English to find steady repair work when not at the stockyards. He conducted business in the surrounding neighborhoods, fixing units for individual homes, restaurants, and grocery stores. Gramps quickly joined his father and together they started a small full-time business.

It was at a local grocery store, one in a chain of four, that Gramps met Grannie.

The stores belonged to her Italian family, which had emigrated from Sicily when she was an infant. Unlike Gramps, Grannie's family came in peaceful times, with the immediate intention of building a wonderful new life in the land of opportunity. They came with a plan and money, and the move proved profitable. In their Italian community, they were considered quite well off and were proud of the veritable empire they had started.

Grannie was positioned at the register the day Gramps came to fix a broken meat freezer. She showed him the unit and laughed sweetly when his hands trembled too much to make the repair. With a shy grin, he suggested she go back to the front of the store because he was too distracted by her beauty.

Grannie's family was furious six months later when the secret couple announced that, not only had they been seeing each other, they were in love and intended to wed. The family protested. They had not endured the exhausting hardships of building their business and wealth only to see their one daughter, their Italian princess, marry a lowly Polish immigrant. Grannie cried and screamed and pleaded and wept, but they would not budge. In the end, Gramps and Grannie whisked themselves away into the night and eloped.

To her family's surprise and relief, within five years of the marriage Gramps had grown his father's business into a company of twenty-five repairmen who could work on a full range of appliances.

By the time Gramps and Grannie's children were in grade school, the company had tripled its employees and serviced all of Chicagoland.

❧

GRAMPS'S EYES RETURNED from his far-off thoughts and he flashed a conspiratorial smile. "So, you're getting a taste for the girls, eh?"

"Yeah. I hung out with a girl this year." I paused.

"Hung out? What does that even mean?"

"Well, I guess…"

I couldn't find the word. But I didn't need to. Gramps let out a roar of manly laughter. "Ah! One of those!" Gramps leaned back in his seat. "I knew a few of that kind when I was younger, too. Girls I would *hang out* with. You wouldn't believe it, but this lake was filled with girls at one point."

Not long after Gramps came to America, his father saved enough to buy a small cabin on Black Bear Lake. He said the thick woods reminded him of Poland and it was the only place that felt like home. At the time, the lake was strewn with a multitude of similar cabins, all filled with jovial families geared up for summer festivities. Our family compound wasn't formed until years later.

"There were many, many girls. They would come from university to spend time during the summer. I would always manage to find some reason to be up here then, too." He winked at me. "Maybe the roof would need repairs. Or maybe some wood needed chopping. It never bothered me to chop wood when the girls were here." Gramps laughed hard again. "Hated it when my father made me do it in Poland, but never here when the girls came for vacation."

Gramps sighed happily. "During the day, after chores, we had swimming contests, diving contests, and foot races. Of course, the girls were smart. They egged us on just enough for us boys to make fools of ourselves. How we showed off! We held a lake-wide talent show every year, you know. Singing, hula dancing, terrible dancing. How we loved those days! Ah, and every night we'd meet out at the beach point for bonfires. We played the ukulele, sang songs, roasted hot dogs"—Gramps smiled wickedly and winked— "and occasionally someone snuck in a bottle of gin. Those were the best nights. The singing got loud and the laughter came so easy. But as I said, the girls were smarter than us."

"What do you mean?"

"They would yawn and say, *Oh, we are tired*, giggling the whole time. Then one sweet peck on the cheek and off they would go for the night." Gramps closed his eyes for a moment and sighed. "The feeling of one light kiss would send me to the moon."

I immediately thought of Amy and realized her presence had brought an exciting new element to our predictable summer routine. I thought of her leg grazing mine under the water. I thought of the kiss in the woods. Gramps was right: It sent me to the moon.

"I even had a special girl for a while." He paused, and then smiled gently. "Nothing like your Grannie, though." Gramps nodded to himself. "It's very nice now being here. With her. With my own family. With children and grandchildren. Yes. It's nice. Nice"—he paused again— "but different."

We sat in silence for a while, his mind in the past, mine in the hopeful future.

"You know"—he continued, a piece of wisdom on the tip of his tongue as he nodded—"God gives you these years, he opens you up, makes you aware of *everything*. Whether you know it or not, the things you are learning right now at *almost* fifteen years old will shape who you become, the decisions you will make, the path you will take." His accent was thick in his throat.

"I saw too much death when I was your age."

Gramps paused and let silence put extra weight on his statement.

"You see, death on the television or some make-believe horror at the movies, it's not true. It's not the same. To see death, to see it in person, to see the soul leaving a body…it changes you."

I had stopped looking at the scenery and found myself staring at a small spot on the car's interior.

"When you experience this, it changes how you see the world. And when you experience this at a young age, at *your* age, it's even more impactful." Gramps looked out the corner of his eye at me. "Do you understand what I'm saying? Death becomes the thing that shapes you."

I watched the trees race past us in a green blur. We sat in silence until Gramps asked sternly, "How are your brothers?"

"Okay, I guess."

"They look up to you?"

"I don't know."

"They listen to you?"

I laughed. "Not at all."

"They'll learn to. You'll be in charge soon."

Blood drained from my face and rushed in my ears.

"Your father will need to work more. For money and for sanity. He'll need a diversion. At least for a while." When I didn't answer, he turned to me. "After you mother passes away."

My throat closed. There was nowhere to turn to and escape. How did he know? Had Mom finally told them?

"You did not think I knew?"

I shook my head.

"Of course, I knew. I told you, I saw death daily for years on end during the war. I can see it a mile away. I can smell it."

I felt sick to my stomach. "I'm not supposed to…I mean, they asked me not to tell…"

Gramps's face softened. "I'm proud of you. You handle it like a man." He blinked hard. "Your Grannie does not know. And she shouldn't. Only when it's over, not before."

Gramps glanced at me and I noticed that his eyes, usually hard and intense, were moist and searching.

"You should know, these women, they are strong. Much stronger than men. They carry a larger burden. They learn to fight, love, battle for their wants and needs, all on men's terms. They learn to be clever. They make themselves the true leaders while you and I just stomp around like angry bulls. Living this way makes them hard. Makes them rocks. They become steel beams that can carry unthinkable weight." He paused. "But not this. This they cannot carry. They cannot lose a child. This we must protect them from. It is our duty, the one thing we can be stronger about. Because when a mother loses a child, a part of her dies, too. That's how entwined mother and child are. Woven together. Men are not the same. Fathers are not the same. But mothers…" He stared straight ahead. "This is why Grannie cannot know. Not yet. You see?"

I nodded and focused on the passing scenery without seeing it. I dug my nails deep into my palm, willing the tears to stay in place. I was petrified Gramps would see the fear and pain on my face. I was afraid I wasn't being the man he thought I was. We drove on in silence and I thought of how losing someone could make a part of you die as well.

Was my mother feeling that now? Knowing she was leaving us, was a part of her already dying? My stomach tightened further, thinking of how we might be pushing her toward the day we all dreaded most. And I knew that it would work the same way for us. We were too young to lose her, and there was no doubt she would take away something priceless when she left. A part of me would die.

It had already begun.

Chapter 11

That night after dinner, the boys' cabin was a veritable zoo full of monkeys. Kevin and the Means moved all the bunk beds to the far sides of the room, clearing a large square space in the center to hold our own version of pro wrestling. The Feathers stumbled in, ready to rumble, full of beer and bravado. They rolled around, holding each other in bumbling bear hugs until their Leinenkugel bottles were empty, then made their way back down to the lodge. The rest of us stayed and, despite the stifling heat, were in frenzy mode. Our laughter and screaming were deafening.

The circle of boys surrounded Kevin and little Justin as they crouched on opposite ends of the room while Tommy, naked as ever, jumped up and down on a bed to catch a view of the chaos. We whooped, mocked, and shouted while simultaneously doling out wrestling advice. The two opponents circled each other, snarling like rabid dogs. Mikey pulled on my T-shirt in excitement and screamed, "Kill him, Kevie! Rip him apart!" I laughed at Mikey's exuberant support and found myself screaming out along with the group.

"Hit him at the knees!"

"You should fight the winner, Adam."

I egged Mikey along. "I don't know. They're pretty tough."

"But you're so much tougher. I bet you could beat anybody in here." He was jumping with excitement. "I bet you could fight ten of them at the same time and you'd win!"

I laughed again and my chest swelled with brotherly pride.

Back in the circle, the two boys charged each other, and the audible smack of their bodies fed our mania. They immediately fell to the ground and began to roll side to side as if caught in a sleeping bag. Neither had the first clue how to wrestle, mimicking instead the dog and pony show they watched on TV. They crashed into a bunk bed and ricocheted into a large group of kids, including me. We were a tangled heap of limbs and blankets and suddenly the wrestling match was no longer between Kevin and Justin. We all became contenders and grabbed whichever arm, leg, or head of hair was closest and pulled it to the ground. We ended as one tangled pile of wriggling worms.

Then the lights went out.

The Minnows shrieked.

"It's just a tripped circuit," I yelled. "I'll go fix it." The kids continued to scream at the top of their lungs, though now with smiles on their faces, simply happy for an excuse to exercise their lungs. "Dudes! Quit screaming," I shouted over my shoulder as I jogged to the back of the cabin. The switchboard was two cabins away in the utility hut. I went inside and, sure enough, the switch to our cabin was off. I flipped it on and could hear the cheers before stepping back out into the heavy, humid air.

Back at the boys' cabin, Kevin and Justin were sprawled on the beds, panting and laughing at each other's rising bruises while Tommy and Mikey were scrapping like puppies.

The lights went out again.

The mock screaming began again, until Tommy let out a very real shout. "What's that?"

From the back window in the cabin, a dark figure rose then fell away. I hung onto my composure and reassured the boys. "Just a shadow. It's probably from one of the trees. Don't freak out. I'll go hit the lights again." The boys jumped around each other and clung to each other's shirts and short bottoms.

I walked out of the cabin with false bravado. The pines rustled in the hot breeze as I made my way back to the cobweb-infested utility hut. I glanced over my shoulder before heading in to flip on the switch but saw little from the dim light of the moon.

Stepping outside of the hut, I could see the lights were on in the cabin. I walked back with a bit more speed.

Once inside, I realized I had held my breath for the short walk over.

Then the lights went out again.

More screams erupted as a shadow fell across a window at the opposite side of the cabin.

This time I didn't pretend to be filled with courage. I opened the door and ran while my legs turned to Jell-O. Although my parents strictly prohibited horror movies, I had snuck out to see *Friday the 13th Part 2* a couple of years earlier while staying the night with a friend. The movie's images were seared in my brain and I fully expected to look back and see Jason marching toward me with a bloodied machete swinging in his hand. I ran into the hut, slipped on pine needles and flipped the switch, barely pausing long enough to see what my fingers touched before running back out. My chest pounded and my thigh muscles started to fail. Just as I reached the cabin, I looked through a window to see the lights flick out again. Through the opposing window, the bulky silhouette of a large bear came into view. One paw rose and methodically scratched at the screen.

Two full seconds of surreal silence passed while I watched in horror.

Then I screamed.

I screamed over and over, hitting a pitch and volume I never knew existed. The terrified screams from inside the cabin began and quickly overtook my own screeching. I was frozen in place, my feet refusing to move forward and save the kids or turn around and hide in the hut. All I could do was scream.

As quickly as it appeared, the shadow of the bear vanished. With that, my feet found wings. I turned on my heels and ran straight for the hut. Sticks jumped up and stabbed my calves and I tripped over logs. Shaking like a leaf, I hid in the corner.

That's when I heard them.

Girls. Giggling girls. Giggling girls running past the hut.

I rose to peep out the door and saw the group, led by Dannie, fleeing into the woods. I quit shaking in fear and began trembling from embarrassment and anger while running to where the bear had been. There were no paw prints or claw marks on the window. Instead, lying on the ground just below was a crude cardboard cutout resembling Old Papa.

The girls' cabin versus boys' cabin pranks had begun.

Chapter 12

T he heat refused to break.

It was too hot for volleyball or tennis and we were
tired enough of sitting in the tepid lake, so it was decided
we would spend the day at the river, floating lazily in canoes
and inner tubes. The Feathers and their significant others
thought the plan was brilliant and immediately began to fill
a large cooler with ice and beer.

It seemed to take hours for the adults to herd the pack
together while a chorus of exclamations sounded
throughout the camp.

"Where is the blue cooler? This one is too small."

"Just use the red one."

"The seal is broken. Where is the blue one?"

"Has anyone seen Tommy's swim trunks?"

"Don't leave without me! I just want to grab something!"

"Justin, please run up to the boys' cabin and grab
Tommy's trunks."

"I found the cooler!"

"Dude! You can't find anything in that cabin! It's a
pigsty!"

"Did someone take my pink-striped beach towel?"

"Go up anyway and see if the trunks are lying out in view.
Take Kevin."

"Seriously, look at the size of this cooler. This isn't the
right one."

"It's blue."

"It's also going to hold a max of four cans. Think, man. Think!"

"A bunch of towels went up to the laundry hut. Look there."

"We have two other coolers that are completely full."

"Kevin won't go to the cabin. He has his seat in the van and he won't give it up."

"I don't want to run out of beer. Do *you* want to run out of beer? I don't think so. Let's find the blue cooler. The big one!"

"Would you get a towel for me, too?"

"Grab the boombox."

"Gross! Who left all the wet towels in the washer and didn't turn it on? The hut smells disgusting now!"

"Dude, I'm not taking my boombox. It's brand new and I don't want it to get ruined."

"Found the cooler! That's right. Who's the man? I'm the man."

"So, we don't have any clean towels?"

"Put the boombox in your canoe. I have the new Psychedelic Furs tape. It's totally awesome!"

"Nice. Now be a real man and go grab the cases of Leinenkugel out of the walk-in fridge."

"This is ridiculous. Where are Tommy's swim trunks?"

Dannie and I leaned against the People Mover, an old, beat up '70s Volkswagen van. Gramps bought it used, then tore out all the back seats and had the floor carpeted. His theory was that without actual seats we could cram in twice the number of passengers. Any major summer outing we took found everyone piled on top of one other, desperately trying to claim a small square of space on the floorboards. The Feathers didn't help the claustrophobic sensation of the van by sneaking it out at night for inebriated visits to the local casino. Without fail, at least one of them would end up vomiting on the carpet during their joy ride. Accentuated by the heat, the lingering smell trapped in unidentifiable patches of crusted carpet was lethal.

Dannie wiped a bead of sweat off her temple. "It's like herding cats."

"Worse. At least cats are cute."

We watched as naked Tommy ran past, screeching, "I don't want to go!" Amy chased close behind. She stopped in front of us, panting. A line of sweat ran down her cleavage. "Fuck it."

"Come on," I said to Dannie, "let's help her or we'll never get out of here."

Fifteen minutes later, we sat on each other's laps in the back of the van, our slick and sweaty bodies too lethargic from the heat to care what parts were being mashed together.

Eric took the driver's seat, his nose and eyes still a kaleidoscope of deep purples and reds from Dannie's spike, while Kevin reigned victorious in the passenger seat. The adults, in a brilliant move, had waited for the van to fill and then declared there was no room left for them. They drove off, waving merrily in their air-conditioned cars.

Angie, settled on top of Terry who sat on top of Matt, took a swig from her beer bottle. "Kevin, how in the hell did you get that seat?"

Kevin grinned obnoxiously. "I'm a badass."

Angie shook her head. "More like an asshole."

Tommy finally jumped into the van, still without swim trunks. He crawled over everyone and wiggled in between Terry and Kevin.

Amy peered into the van and then tiptoed precariously over protesting bodies until she came to a stop.

On my lap.

"Do you mind?" She grinned at me, then pulled a giggling Dannie onto her own lap.

"Hey! I'm being crushed," I protested.

"Want me to move?" Amy's face was no more than an inch from mine.

I swallowed hard and forced myself to reply as nonchalantly as possible. "Not if…um…no."

Eric glanced back in the rearview mirror, "Nice seat ya got there, Adam!"

A cheer let out from the group, and I marveled at how Amy ate up the attention, not the least bit self-conscious.

We traveled on, the van and its apparent lack of shocks bumping and throwing us about with every pothole, each time causing Amy to sink deeper into my cross-legged lap. I tried desperately to distract myself, but there was no escaping how well we fit together and how tantalizing each bump of the van felt.

In the dark, the closeness of our bodies and my assumption that no one was watching gave me a wave of courage. Slowly, I allowed my arm to slide up and wrap around Amy's waist. To my amazement, and relief, she reciprocated by leaning back into my chest. With her back to me, my eyes scanned her silhouette, starting from the top of her head. Her full mane of hair, her long swan neck, her lean, tight back, and narrow waist.

We sat in stillness and talked in whispers. The air was thick with Coppertone, and when the thoughts that seemed to follow these quiet moments began creeping into my head—thoughts of Mom, of my brothers, of the shell Dannie was developing—I held Amy tighter.

A shock ran through me when I felt her hand slide onto my thigh, her thumb softly rubbing my skin. I was momentarily frozen with fear that Dannie would see. But as I realized we had no attention on us, I let go. I didn't care about the heat, didn't care we were in the van surrounded by other people, didn't care about the somber thoughts that were knocking at the door of my mind.

I didn't care about anything.

WE REACHED THE canoe landing and checked in with the river guides. The camp hired college kids to run the program and, as long as no one drowned, the kids did not enforce any camp rules such as no alcohol, loud music, or horseplay, which is why the older cousins loved it. As greetings were exchanged between family members and longtime camp workers, we began pairing off for the ride. Canoes and tubes were sent down the river one by one, the current so slow it would take a good four hours to make it down to the end dock. The boombox blared Depeche Mode, and most of the Feathers were well into their beer buzz before shoving off.

Dannie and I decided to canoe together and to go last, right after Amy and Tommy. It was the only way to have a private conversation without constant interruptions and prodding from the others. We had learned from many previous excursions that only staying as far away as possible could ensure a peaceful ride.

Amy stepped down into her canoe and reached up to help Tommy, who leaped instead and hit the canoe off center, flipping over the whole thing. Amy and Tommy sailed into the water with a shriek.

"Goddammit, Tommy!" she yelled, then grabbed him under his armpits as he thrashed and gulped in river water. She swam to the shore, dumping Tommy on the bank. Dannie and I ran to where she fumed.

Amy's white tank top was nearly see-through, and she had not prepared for getting in the water.

"Yikes. No suit, huh?" Dannie smiled, leaving out her lack of a bra, too. "We should probably take care of that. Come on, you can wear my T-shirt. I've got my suit on under." They went up the hill to the camp bathroom and I meandered back to the loading dock to wait with Tommy.

"Guess what I am!" Tommy yelled and hunched his back, swinging one arm in front of him.

"I don't know."

"An elephant! Now guess what I am." He pursed his lips and pretended to swim. I realized this would go on until the girls returned, so I humored him.

"A parrot?"

Tommy fell to the ground laughing, "No! I'm a fish. Now what am I?"

This went on for several more minutes. If we didn't get started down the river soon, we would lose our group altogether. It was one thing to stay a good distance back, but it was another to be completely alone if we ran into any trouble. I walked toward the bathroom.

As I rounded the corner to the entrance door, Amy tumbled out, followed closely by Dannie. Amy had on Dannie's bikini top, while Dannie wore her loose T-shirt. I was struck by how different Dannie's bikini looked on Amy, who smiled brightly. She threw one arm around my waist and the other around Dannie's. "Much better."

"Cool. We should get going." It took all my effort to form the words while my mind buzzed with sexual energy.

With the rest of the group so far ahead, our ride was sleepy. Tommy sat in front of Amy in their canoe, bouncing in his seat and paddling to save his life while humming a TV cartoon anthem. Amy sat with the paddle on her lap. When we laughed at this, she smiled. "Hey, maybe this will finally wear him out."

Our canoes drifted in silence while the heat beat down through the riverbank's towering pines. The trees were beginning to turn brown around the edges, evidence the sun and lack of rain were taking their toll. The river ahead was like glass except when an occasional minnow jumped out of the water attempting to escape a walleye or carp.

Dannie and I took turns rowing, exerting just enough energy to propel us forward, but no more. I didn't mind and found a small, barely conscious comfort in the rhythm of the strokes. Every now and then, Dannie looked back at me and smiled.

With Dannie, I could breathe.

Amy had so much energy circling her, and my nerve endings stood on end when I was around her, preparing for the next adrenaline shot. But being with Dannie was the same as being alone with my thoughts, as if we melded into one. I didn't get hot prickles down my legs or become painfully self-conscious around her. I didn't try to impress her and never felt the need to give gratuitous praise. There were no highs or lows with Dannie. We just were.

She leaned back and looked up at the sky, then rolled her head lazily to the side and looked at Amy.

"What are you going to do after school?"

Amy sighed. "That's the million-dollar question."

"Are you going to college?"

"Not unless I win the lottery."

College was a subject I was well versed in. In our family, attending college was not a question. My parents talked about it ad nauseam. The main concern, of course, was money. But they agreed to find a way, by whatever means necessary. Whether it was their small savings, scholarships, or a combination of all, it would happen.

"What about student loans?" Dannie asked.

"I don't want to be tied to anybody. If I take a loan, whether it's from a bank, college, or friends, it means I have to stick around to pay it back." She shook her head. "I want my freedom to fly whenever I want."

"Scholarship?"

Amy snorted and stared off. "I don't even know if I'll graduate. I'm thinking of skipping out soon."

Dannie's eyes widened. "But you're only sixteen. I mean, you only have two years left. Why wouldn't you finish?"

"I'm thinking of going to LA."

Dannie sat back up. "I thought you were going to stay in Chicago?"

"Maybe. I don't know. I think I want to be on a TV show. Or maybe be in a movie."

"Is it that easy?" I couldn't keep the doubt out of my voice. "Have you ever done any acting?"

Amy shrugged. "No. But really, how hard is it? I mean, it's pretty much a bunch of people who get done up by a make-up artist and are filmed being beautiful, right?"

We floated on and enjoyed the passing scenery. In the distance, whoops of laughter and friendly chaos floated across the water as the Feathers merrily made their way through the cooler of beer.

"What about you, Edgar Allen Poe? Do you know what you want to do?"

I did. I made my plans early. And considering my immediate family, that plan was not surprising.

"I'll go to UIC, get my teaching degree, then someday I really want to be an English professor there."

"Tweed jacket and everything?"

"Haha. Very funny."

Dannie smiled. "I think it's nice. I can totally picture you." She turned to face forward and began rowing again. "You'll have a cozy office filled with books. Probably filled with doe-eyed co-eds, too. Then you'll pack up your papers into a beat-up messenger at the end of the day, hop on a bicycle, and ride to your little row house filled with Tiffany lamps, bookshelves, and a golden retriever." She paused and smiled at me again. "It fits you."

I blushed. She knew me inside out.

Amy eyed me skeptically. "But don't you want to get out? I mean, you grew up in Chicago."

"Maybe I'll travel some."

"But you really think you'll go back to Chicago?"

"Yeah. I do. It's a great place to be a writer and UIC is where I want to be. Plus, I want to be close to my family." I didn't want to add that I had no choice in the matter. At some point, I'd be taking on responsibilities and obligations that would require me to be in the same city or neighborhood as my family. The same house, most likely.

Amy's tone was somber. "I can't imagine what that would be like, to want to stay anywhere for long." She turned to me, her eyes piercing. "Don't you ever feel tied down? Trapped?"

I shook my head, so Amy turned away and stared at the trees on the bank. How could I tell her that yes, I felt trapped. I *was* trapped. And that admitting that I had no choice, that my fate felt utterly sealed, seemed like an unforgivable betrayal to Mom and Dad, who had it even worse. Although Amy professed the need for freedom, I wondered how lonely a small apartment with only her father must be. I wondered if she, deep down, longed to feel tied down.

"You want to come over for dinner sometime when we get back to Chicago?" I asked. "Maybe before school starts again?"

Amy smirked. "You mean like a date?"

"No. I mean, with my family. A family dinner."

"I'd like that." She looked up the river and smiled again, nodding to herself. "Dinner with family. With you."

Dannie turned away and began to paddle again, this time with more force.

❧

WHEN WE ARRIVED back at camp, Amy ran ahead, chasing down Tommy while Dannie and I wandered up the blue stone path. We were sunburned and exhausted from rowing. Dannie had sunk into a fit of icy silence that I was trying to decipher. I secretly hoped she would take Amy up on the offer to stay with her in Chicago. I began to have fleeting fantasies of us spending time together, inseparable, the Three Musketeers. But Dannie's flaring moods, which seemed related to Amy or me—I didn't know which or why—introduced a level of drama I didn't understand or know how to deal with.

As we shuffled on up the hill, my confusion at her anger grew with each step. I was about to voice my frustration when shouts, coming from Dannie's parents' cabin, filled every molecule in the air around us.

"Do you have no shame?"

"Why is it shameful to share my dreams with your family?"

"Because you're not sharing dreams. You're asking for money. And you are embarrassing me. Why can't you understand that?"

"The problem is you don't support my vision."

"What vision? Honestly. You got fired because you're a lazy, alcoholic sloth. You didn't get another job—not that you really looked—so you decided it would be more fun to go golfing than to actually earn a living and take care of your family."

"Your family put those words in your mouth. Besides, why should I worry about busting my ass for some mouthy bullshit union leader? You make a great living and there is *no way* you're ever going to get fired."

"What does that mean?"

"That means why would Fineburg mess up a good thing?"

"What are you implying?"

"Nothing. It's just strange that you're the only one who ever stays late to work with him."

"Dennis is my boss. That's it. Besides, I *have* to stay late because we need the extra money."

"Well, I guess you got the means to earn it, one way or another."

It was hard to make out Dannie's expression in the fading light. She stood stiffly, motionless, staring into the darkness. I wanted to reach out to her. I wanted to grab her hand, to hug her, to whisk her away. But somehow I knew it wasn't the first time she'd experienced this argument, and no matter how much I tried to shelter her, it wouldn't be the last.

"How dare you? Dennis has never laid a finger on me. He knows I am a faithful woman, and our relationship is strictly professional. Unlike the umpteen waitress *friends* I could name down at Skippy's. That's right, I know about them. I also know all about the hairdresser, and the hostess at Tomfooleries, and the dental assistant."

There was a small pause, and I could hear Patty trying to stifle a sob.

"You spying on me now?"

"That's what you're fixated on? How I know? No, I haven't been spying on you. It's not like you've been trying to hide it. Do you know how humiliating it is to have my friends seeing this…this *shit* you do, and then report it all back to me? Like they're doing me a favor?"

"Then why don't you leave?"

"Because we have a daughter, you jerk! Otherwise I'd have left a long time ago. Believe me."

With that, Dannie took off at breakneck speed.

"Dannie!"

She didn't stop. Didn't pause. Didn't look back.

Dannie was fleeing.

Chapter 13

D inner that night was uncommonly quiet as the float trip had stripped away everyone's energy reserves. Gramps and Grannie ate early with the Minnows and Means, and the adults who waited until the later dinner bell were paired off, engaged in quiet chats.

I served myself a plate of roasted chicken thighs, butter-soaked corn on the cob, and topped it with overcooked green beans before walking with stiff, sunburned arms to the dining room.

Dad and Richard sat at a corner table, hunched over a piece of paper in deep discussion, no doubt astounded by some new scientific discovery or act of political backlash. Mom hadn't come down for dinner, but quickly pushed aside any worry. I wasn't surprised that Patty, Ron, and Dannie were also missing. I debated whether to check in on Dannie, but the premonition of an awkward conversation in which I tried and failed to think of anything to say made the decision easy.

Kevin sat with a small group of Means, and I watched for a moment as they blew wads of green beans out of straws at each other. I decided to sit with the Feathers.

"Don't be such a dickhead," said Tabitha, Terry's girlfriend who we had all met for the first time that day. She slurred her words and tried to focus both eyes.

"Tabby, why don't you switch to water for a while?" Terry said through bites of chicken.

"See? That's exactly what I'm talking about. You're always telling me what to do." She swayed slightly.

Angie rolled her eyes. "That has nothing to do with what you were talking about."

Terry shot Angie a look. "Not helping." He passed his water glass to Tabitha. "Here, take mine."

Tabitha tried to focus on Angie. "So, what *was* I talking about, Miss Know It All?"

"You were pissed because he didn't tell you that you looked pretty when you came in for dinner." Angie eyed with disdain Tabitha's smudged mascara and cocktail-stained dress. "Which may have been a message in itself," she mumbled.

The group around the table muffled their guffaws and Katie patted a seat next to her, motioning me over. "Come on. The show's almost over. We hope, anyway."

I set my plate down as Tabitha pushed away from the table. Her chair teetered for a moment on its back legs, then righted itself. She stumbled out of the dining room and shouted over her shoulder. "Dickhead!"

From out of nowhere, Gramps voice bellowed, "Control your woman, Terry!"

The rest of us exchanged glances for a moment, then erupted in laughter as Terry shook his head until embarrassment dissolved into a snicker.

Angie hiccupped between cackling. "What a train wreck."

"Hey, don't say that. She's the love of my life." Terry fluttered his eyes mockingly.

Paul laughed hard. "She's the flavor of the month. Don't confuse the two."

Eric hugged his girlfriend, Rena. "Thank goodness some of us have both in one." She punched his arm playfully.

"And a good flavor she is, from what I hear." Terry wiggled his eyebrows and again the cousins roared merrily.

It was strange and exhilarating to sit and talk so openly about sex, with no moral to the story's end. No horror story about teen pregnancy or how herpes is for life. There was no uncomfortable shame attached. It was surprisingly freeing.

Eric smiled through his swollen nose, "I'm serious. That's not a bad thing, is it? To love someone *and* be attracted to them?"

Rena smiled and nuzzled his cheek.

The words came out of my mouth before I could stop them. "But what do you get out of it?"

The table froze. Forks stopped mid-air and glasses were held to lips without drinking.

Eric cleared his throat and looked at me with amusement. "How's that?"

I stumbled, suddenly not sure of what I was saying. "I guess, um, I mean, what do you get out of the love and attraction?"

Knowing smiles circled the table. Katie ruffled my hair. "Something tells me you haven't been in love before."

Angie smirked. "Or had sex. Because you wouldn't have to ask." Everyone chuckled and whistled as I sank deep into my chair.

Terry took a swig of beer. "Speaking of Adam and love, how's your girlfriend holding up?"

My face caught fire. I hadn't told anyone about my feelings towards Amy, and I was positive no one had been aware of our slow advances.

"Jesus, did you hear Ron and Patty?" The table moaned, and I realized the *girlfriend* they were talking about was Dannie.

Paul shook his head. "Who *didn't* hear? I was down in one of the boats by the end of the dock and I heard them."

Angie looked at me from under her teased bangs. "Is she okay?"

I shrugged. "She took off. I haven't seen her since this afternoon."

"I don't blame her. It sucks." Eric put his arm around Rena. "That fucking Ron is such an asshole."

"Eric..."

"No, I mean it. He doesn't financially support his family and, judging by these screaming matches, he's crazy and abusive. Not to mention he has hit on every single one of our girls up here for the last five years. Babysitters included."

My ears prickled.

Angie made an overly large eye gesture in my direction.

"No, it's okay," Eric said, looking directly at me. "No one knows that family better than Adam, right? Maybe no one talks about it, but that doesn't mean it's not happening. Or that it's not true. Patty and Dannie would be better off without him. Our whole family would."

Eric was right. I did know Dannie better than anyone. So how could I not have put all of this together? I had simply taken for granted that Ron acted the way he did, just because he did. It didn't occur to me the situation could change. That it *should* change. I never viewed Dannie or Patty as being abused—that's just the way it was. And I'd never considered how I would feel if it was Dad who belittled me or never brought home a paycheck or spent his time at bars with other women. I was suddenly confused about why Dannie would keep this all inside and not confide in me. But I was more frustrated that I didn't see it sooner.

"Soooooo…" Karen smiled at Eric and changed the subject "Big man on campus this year, huh?"

"That's right. And whooooo, I'm ready to be done."

"You can't be done yet. Phi Gam's Fiji Island this year, dude. You promised you'd come."

"Oh, I wanted to go to that, too. What's the date? I want you guys to come to our game against Michigan. Our tailgate is totally awesome."

Listening to the conversation made the dark thoughts of Dannie's family disappear. Their warmth, jovial ribbing, lighthearted plans for the future. It was like a warm blanket, the thought of our group visiting each other, supporting each other, and sharing with each other.

But deep in the recesses of my mind, I felt a tug of melancholy. I was here with them, but not a part of them. My part, my blanket, was somewhere in a cabin crying alone. She was unable to share with me, couldn't let me be her security. And that left me alone as well. We only had each other. But right now, we had no one.

I cleared my plate and wove through unruly children and the boisterous laughs of inebriated adults, feeling more and more isolated.

In the kitchen, a mountainous pile of dishes threatened to topple over as Amy alone bent over the sink scrubbing.

"Hey there." I said. "Why are you doing the dishes?"

"Kids' night for kitchen duty. Basically, that means babysitters clean up." She smiled weakly. "I needed a break from Tommy, so I told the others if they'd take the kids away, I'd do all the dishes. They took the scrap bucket out to feed the pigs." She looked around. "It's actually kind of peaceful."

"Want some company?"

Amy smiled at me and tossed a towel in my direction. "Where's Dannie?"

I shrugged, trying to give off an air of indifference. "She doesn't like me."

"Yes, she does. She's just dealing with some…shit." I let the explicative roll off my tongue to see how it felt.

"I want her to like me." She glanced over my shoulder. "I want the family to like me." She looked me square in the eye. "I want you to like me." She ran a slightly damp hand gently over my face. Her fingertips had soap suds on them, and she outlined my cheeks, nose, and lips. Her smile left me breathless.

Turning back to the dishes, we worked side by side for an hour. She spoke softly as she asked countless questions about my past, wanting stories, not answers. She smiled as I recounted sibling rivalries, holiday gatherings, births, and deaths. She never mentioned any of her own.

Amy tilted her head towards me while her hands hovered over the sink, dripping wet. "You have a beautiful life. Do you know that?" I nodded, embarrassed. She turned back to the sink, her eyes glazed over in thought. "I'd do anything to have the stories you have. The people you have. Your life."

When we finished, Amy glanced up at the wall clock.

"Wow. I better put Tommy to bed."

I nodded but wanted nothing less in the world than for her to move away from our spot at the sink.

"Are you going to go to the bonfire?"

"Yeah, I guess. Maybe not. I mean, Dannie's probably not going to be there, and if you're with Tommy…"

She took a step closer to me and whispered. "Wait up for me."

I prayed my legs wouldn't give out as she turned to leave.

The next two hours lasted an eternity. Several people stayed up reminiscing, fueled by warm beer and a poorly hidden joint the Feathers passed around. They giggled, jabbed, and hugged, but I noticed little else as my eyes continually jumped to the pathway with every passing shadow.

Finally, Amy emerged.

She had changed from Dannie's tee to a small tank and *very* short shorts, her long tan legs gleaming as they reflected the bonfire's glow.

Without a word, she passed behind me and tugged slightly at the back of my shirt. I quickly stood and followed, thankful to leave the intoxicated love-fest unnoticed.

We walked in complete silence. I followed ten paces behind her until we rounded the beach to a remote area lit only by moonlight.

She halted with her back to me and took off her top. As she looked out towards the lake, Amy arched her back and stretched her arms high above her head. All I could do was stare at her flawless skin. It shone silver, the same as the moon, her curves accentuated and magnified by the shadows. She pulled off her shorts, then slowly moved towards the lake with no self-consciousness whatsoever. Waist deep in the water, she finally turned to me and smiled.

I realized she wanted me to follow and quickly threw off my polo, shorts, and boxers in a thoughtless frenzy. I was knee-deep in the water before the temperature registered.

"Cold?" Amy laughed.

I nodded, completely mortified and utterly grateful for the surrounding darkness.

"Just get in quick," she chirped. I obeyed, dunked my body, and shivered violently. Amy smiled again.

"Now, come with me."

We waded out farther, then quietly swam to the floating dock and climbed up on the far side, away from the beach. We could have been alone on a deserted island. Amy and I lay on our backs and again I shivered, either from the cold water evaporating off my body or the adrenaline rush of what was happening.

Amy didn't say a word as she turned to me and touched my lips. I could barely make out her face, save for her glistening eyes and silky curves. There was a hush on the lake and my breaths seemed unnaturally loud and raspy. I couldn't get enough air in my lungs to settle my heart.

Like a serpent, she slithered onto me. I was astonished how smooth she was and how she moved around me without awkwardness. No elbow jabs. No bumping noses. Tentatively, I put my hands on her back and tried to maneuver myself to fit her position. She leaned in close to my ear and whispered, "Let me show you."

Tangled limbs and slippery skin transported me.

My mind went blank, and I didn't think. I didn't think about Dannie. I didn't think about Mom. I didn't think about my fears for the future, my family, my school. For the first time in a long while, there were no hidden layers of sadness, only exhilaration and joy, ecstasy and rapture.

Then it rushed in. Not a spark of light, but the entire spectrum of color. My world of letters, sentences, and structure meant to explain every thought and feeling came crashing down.

For the first time, there were no words.

Chapter 14

I woke mid-morning. My vision of the cabin interior rippled in the heat. The large open room was empty as I sprawled on the bed, stared at the ceiling, and marveled at the night before.

Everything was different.

I was different.

I wanted to jump out of bed and run screaming, announcing to everyone I passed of my great discovery. I wanted to run to Gramps and tell him everything, have him pat me on the back and shake my hand, call me a *man*. I wanted to sit at dinner with my older cousins and nod, maybe wink, when they talked about sex, signal that I knew what they were talking about.

The thought of telling Dannie stopped my daydream. Somehow it felt wrong, although I couldn't quite comprehend why. It made me question the act itself. But as quickly as the notion entered my head, I banished it and returned to languishing in my triumph. I stretched tall and decided not to shower off the exotic fragrance of Amy. Of us. Pulling out my notebook, I wrote frantically. It was like a dam had opened and a world of feelings I'd never known poured out. I smiled reading my new inner confessions, then headed to the lodge, ravenous.

The Minnows ran amuck while Kevin and the Means were full into King of the Mountain on the floating dock. Mikey was burying Tommy in the sand, only his head sticking out while Mikey formed two mounding breasts on his coffin as both boys laughed hysterically.

Then it hit me. I yelled out to Eric and Terry, who were gathering up fishing rods and tackle gear. "Where are all the girls?"

Paul came around a corner, toting a cooler for their fishing excursion. "Interrogation." He nodded towards the lodge.

I quietly slipped into the lodge's back screen door and found my female cousins scattered around the living room, both Minnows and Means. Tammy sat in front of the fireplace, flanked by Mom and Patty, like royalty in front of their subjects. The girls varied in expressions of boredom, fear, and confusion. A young cousin shot her hand up in the air.

"Yes, Caroline?" Patty asked wearily.

"But what about the boys? Their cabin's a lot messier."

"Not according to the smell," Tammy said tersely.

I scanned the room and found Dannie. She was curled up in an oversized chair, picking absently at the frayed tapestry depicting a fox hunt scene in progress. She glanced up and caught my eye, pulled a face, and waved me over.

Another girl piped up. "They always have spilled pop and chips in theirs and you never yell at *them*."

Mom sighed. "Girls, we're not yelling at you. But the smell is atrocious. In fact, this all came about because *you* came to *us* saying you couldn't stand the fumes anymore, correct?"

I quickly dipped behind the chair and slid in next to Dannie. She threw her legs over mine to accommodate our bodies. "Where have you been?" she whispered.

"Asleep."

"It's noon."

"I was up late."

"Yeah, I know."

I paused, not sure what she meant or knew. Part of me desperately wanted to share what had happened, but in truth, a larger part felt it would spark another mood swing.

"I went into the cabin last night and it stank, so I went to sleep in Amy's cabin with the babysitters. She got in late and said you guys stayed up talking on the dock."

I swallowed to drain any hint of emotion from my voice. "Oh, yeah. We did." She smiled at me with such serene innocence, I knew she didn't think anything more of it. I left it that way. "So, what's this all about?" I nodded at Tammy, who had shut down another protest about the boys' cabin.

"Like I said, our cabin smells like shit. Literally."

"Gross."

"Totally. So now we're all getting lectured about cleanliness and hygiene and picking up our trash and how we're civilized human beings and not the pigs out at the pens and blah blah blah." Dannie rolled her eyes.

"So, what's the smell?"

"Who knows? We're pigs!" She smiled brightly.

Tammy stood up. "After lunch, we will all meet at the cabin and do a complete cleaning. And I mean everyone. Understand?"

There was a collective groan and protests about missing the afternoon activities.

Mom stood next to Tammy. "Girls, this is no light matter. From what I hear, the smell is extremely bad. I don't think any of you want to wake and find Old Papa sniffing around your bunks, do you?" The room fell silent. "I didn't think so. We'll see you up there immediately after lunch."

The room emptied out toward the dining room, while Dannie I headed to the beach. She stretched her arms out and sighed loud. "Thank God that's over."

"Dannie." We turned to see Patty standing at the screen door. "Make sure this doesn't happen again."

"I didn't do it." She said evenly.

"I expect you to be in charge and manage that cabin. You're the oldest one there and when things like this happen, it's a reflection of you," Patty said coldly.

Dannie, without moving a muscle, stared her down. Finally, Patty turned and went back into the lodge.

"Jeez," I muttered.

We continued walking to the beach and saw Kevin throw King of the Mountain competitors off the floating dock.

"Hey guys?" he yelled to the Means. "Do you smell something?" They screeched with laughter. Something about the glint in Kevin's eyes told us both he was behind the mysterious smell in the cabin. Dannie raced down the beach to the shoreline and shouted, "It was you? You did that?"

Kevin shrugged his shoulders in mock confusion. "Did what? I took a shower today. It's not me that stinks."

Dannie glared at Kevin as he doubled over laughing like a hyena, then turned her steely dagger stare towards me.

"I don't know what he did," I said defensively, aware she was ready to release her fury at the nearest target. She turned and stormed off. "Asshole."

Feeling a surge of maturity from the previous night's activities, I decided not to let her get away with punishing me for something I had no part of.

"Dannie," I yelled, holding my ground. I waited, but she kept walking up the blue stone path.

I called out again and tried to deepen my voice, but she disappeared into the trees as she turned a corner on the path. I sighed and ran after her. "Dannie, stop!" She sped up and headed into the woods, straight to the clearing where we rested so peacefully only the week before.

She crossed the opening into the woods, stomped over the bed of moss upon which I had previously rested my head. The sunlight streamed down on her, and I could see hot fury rising from her body.

"I didn't know they were going to do anything. It's just a stupid cabin prank, that's all." I stopped in the clearing, frustrated at her silence.

As she came to the tree line, Dannie stopped and kicked a Jack Pine. I cringed for her toes, only protected by a flimsy flip flop as they hit the tree trunk full force. She kicked the tree again and pulled back a visibly bloody foot. She stood inches from the pine and screamed. She screamed harshly, angrily, pitifully, as she emptied out her lungs. Frozen, I watched the anger, the frustration, the deep sorrow she had swallowed over the summer spew out of her body as she attacked the tree. When Dannie pulled up her foot again, I snapped to attention and ran to her.

I grabbed Dannie's arms and pulled her back. Her foot barely missed as she ripped her arm from my grasp and flung herself against the tree, sliding down the pine's rough bark, tearing her back as she crumbled to the ground, sobbing. She looked up and it frightened me, how broken she seemed.

I fell to the ground next to her with no idea what to do.

"What is going on with you?" I panted with fear.

She stared off into empty space as if I wasn't there and shuddered with each new sob.

"Your mom's not going to stay mad. It was just a prank."

Dannie looked at me and shook her head as large tears streamed down her face.

"You have no idea." She was barely audible and hiccupped with another sob. "You have no idea."

"What?" I was desperate with worry.

"Everything. It's so bad."

We sat until Dannie settled into a slow, steady, quiet cry. I scooted over, our backs to the tree, shoulder to shoulder.

She finally rubbed her face with her palms. Her dirty hands left large streaks across her wet cheeks. Words began to tumble out of her mouth, patternless and disjointed.

"It's…it's….oh, shit, I don't even know what it is, Adam. It was bad at the beginning, or at least I thought it was bad. But now I look at everything going on around me, around my stupid fucked up life, and I think I was crazy, because now I think things weren't so bad then. And it scares me because if I thought it was really bad then, and it got so much worse, then maybe it can get even worse than it is now. And I don't know how I can make it through that."

I stared at her bloody toes. I didn't know how to respond as she continued.

"When Mom and Dad first started fighting, they were like two cats slinking around the house, ignoring each other. Then for some reason their fur would bristle, they'd screech and make swipes at each other, then they would slink away again. They'd try to hide it in front of me, try to pretend everything was fine. But I knew it wasn't. I mean, the air was just so tense when they were together, but we all played along with fake smiles and stupid meaningless conversations about how the day had gone, like either of them cared about anything. It was a relief when they stopped pretending. It was easier. We went through a period where there was no talking at all in the house. They would avoid each other completely, which meant they avoided me too, by default." She paused, lost in her thoughts, and then said to herself. "They left me all alone. Even when we shared the same space, were in the same room, I was alone."

Tears welled up again. "Then it got really nasty. Dad was turned down for jobs so many times that he just stopped looking. Mom was putting in overtime, Dad was drinking a lot, and they started fighting whenever they were in the house at the same time. So Dad started leaving when Mom would come home from work. Some nights he didn't come home until way after she had gone to bed, some nights he didn't come home at all. He was going out to bars and"— she stopped and looked at me sideways, gauging my reaction—"I wish I didn't know where he stayed, but I did. So did Mom. And that made the fights worse. It just became this vicious circle that spun into a cyclone. Dad would leave, go out drinking and…whatever…and then when he actually did come home, he'd sleep until noon because he'd been up all night, which meant that by the time he was awake and had finally gotten rid of his hangover, it was afternoon, and he wouldn't have looked for a job. Then Mom would get home and he'd leave again for the night." She picked up a leaf and began tearing it apart, small bit by small bit. "That's when they stopped ignoring each other and started fighting and screaming. About *everything*. They'd fight over Dad not working. They'd fight because Mom was working late. They'd fight over Dad not coming home, where he was when he wouldn't come home, the bills they couldn't pay…" She started to cry again, choking on her words. "And I didn't have anyone to talk to."

"Your friends must have known something was up? Why didn't you talk to them?" Deep down, a nagging voice wondered why she hadn't called me.

She replenished her tears and looked away. "What friends?"

I almost laughed. As long as I could remember, Dannie had been the All-American, the darling, the It Girl. When I visited her in California, I always watched in awe at how many friends would drop by her house or meet her at the beach for a late-night bonfire. Most times when I would call her, she had to call me back, either because she was running out to meet friends at the mall or because she was surfing with a group she had met the night before. Simply put, everyone loved her.

But the pain on Dannie's face instantly wiped away my conviction.

She wouldn't face me. Instead, she talked to the sky with her eyes closed while tears streamed down her face. "We have no money, Adam."

"We don't have much either, but I still have friends."

"No, it's not the same. It's different in California. It matters. And we don't have *much money*, we have *no* money." She scooped up the sandy dirt and began to sift it back and forth between her hands. "I haven't had any new clothes in over a year and a half. And I'm growing. Mom tries to bring home as many used things as she can get from friends, but even then, they're usually pretty worn out." She scooped another handful. "I showed up one day in a sweater mom had brought home. I was so excited because it had a small hole in the elbow but besides that it was really pretty. It was this awesome pink background with green triangles, and I had even seen Downtown Julie Brown wearing the same one. The morning I put it on, I felt so good. I couldn't stop smiling. I hadn't felt like that in a long time."

She paused. "So, I walk to my locker...and this *bitch*, Lindsay Kirkland, stops right in front of me, with all her friends standing there and says, *Oh wow. I think that's my old sweater! Oh yeah, see? There's that hole in it. That's right, I remember my mom saying she was totally going to give away a bunch of my old stuff to the needy.* And then she made this stupid fake sympathetic face and said, *Let me know if you need some other stuff, too. Like maybe some new jeans? It's really ok because I have so many clothes.* Then she turned around to walk off and I heard her say under her breath to her friends, *Gag.*"

Dannie flung the rest of the dirt from her hand with such force that I jumped.

"And I can't play sports anymore, or cheer."

"Why not?"

"I can't afford it."

"There's no way your mom is making you quit all that stuff. She knows how much it means to you."

"She doesn't know." She finally faced me and shook her head. "I quit on my own. I didn't tell her. I mean, how could I ask for money for a new uniform or team meals when we can't even pay our electric bill?"

"Doesn't she get suspicious when you don't ask her to go to games?"

"She's too preoccupied to even notice." Dannie breathed in deep, and I saw the resignation and defeat in her eyes. "I get off the school bus in the afternoon and start walking. Most of the time I go to the library. I used to go to the mall and walk around, but then it started to make me feel even more alone. Maybe it was all the kids hanging out together or seeing so many stores filled with things I'll never have. But I like the library. I have a quiet little corner I go to every day. I do my homework and then pick out some magazines. When I'm done with that, I pick out a book and read until closing time. Then I walk home and go to bed." She gave me a sad smile. "At least the librarians like me."

We sat in silence and watched hot wind rustle the leaves above us. When I turned to Dannie, she faced me straight on. Her eyes were intense, and the tears reappeared.

"I'm so sorry, Adam. I'm really sorry."

"Why are you sorry? You haven't done anything," I said incredulously.

A dam opened, and her words came quick. "I'm sorry I've been mean to you. I hear myself and I see what I'm doing and it's like I'm watching it from far away. Like I'm watching someone else acting out and I don't have any control over it. I'm sorry I snapped at you about the prank. I know it's just a stupid game and we all do it and it's not personal but...but when I felt like you had been a part of it, and I was getting in trouble and then you didn't even care... I'm so tired of being teased and it felt like I was being teased and…I just…I felt so alone. And I'm really tired of feeling alone." She sobbed and grasped for my hand. Her pleading stare penetrated deep into me. "I need you right now. I know that sounds so stupid and I feel like such a dork saying it. But you have to promise me, Adam. Please make a promise to me."

I was frightened by her intensity and by a situation that seemed so hopeless. I was trying to digest everything she had told me, and my head spun wildly.

"Anything. What do you want me to promise?"

"Don't leave me. Promise you won't leave me. Please." She rolled toward me and threw her face into my chest. She clung to my shirt like a child as I held her tight.

"I promise. I won't leave you."

And more than anything else in my life, that was the truth.

Chapter 15

Dannie and I floated motionless on inner tubes in the sickly tepid water. My thoughts, as they had for two days, bounced back and forth like a pinball between Amy and Dannie and my mother. My heart hurt for Dannie, for Mom, for the state of my future, and I knew these were large, life-altering events. Yet Amy's body cast a soft fog over everything, like a haze-inducing drug. My world of Tessa and frightened exploration seemed light-years behind me, and I felt a strange surge of accomplishment, of passing over some untold hurdle.

Dannie languidly took my hand just as her tube began to drift away from the dock. "I think I'm going to do it."

"What?" My left foot sat in the water, my right on the dock as a tether.

"Move to Chicago. With Amy."

"Man, that would be cool. It would be the three of us all the time."

Dannie smiled, her eyes closed to the glaring sun. "Wouldn't it?"

"What do you think your mom will say?"

"I doubt she'd even notice. Who cares anyway? I may just pack a bag and leave. Not even tell her."

I sat up a little to look at her. "You mean like run away?"

"Not really run away. Just go. It wouldn't be much different than it is now. I don't need much. And I don't have much. Besides, it's not like I'd be living on the street. I'd be with Amy, and your family will be right there, too."

"I guess." A knot formed in my stomach.

Dannie began paddling in. "I'm starving."

"Know what sounds good? A cheese sandwich." I smirked.

Dannie stuck her tongue out and feigned a gag.

After a thorough search, the source of the mystery smell in the girls' cabin was found. Wedged into one of the roof rafters, Tammy discovered a block of blue cheese that the boys had shoved into place and left to ferment. To the delight of all the cousins, Dannie had swiftly tracked down Kevin and forced a bite of the sour, molded, marbled cheese into his mouth.

As we neared the shore, a large cheer erupted from the backyard. Dannie and I quickly made our way around to investigate. I nearly bowled Dannie over when she stopped.

I began to protest, but then spied the spectacle in front of us.

From the top of the blue stone pathway, leading all the way down the steep hill to the bottom of the yard, were twelve mattresses laid end-to-end. At the bottom, the Feathers sat in lawn chairs, Leinenkugel beers in one hand and various poster boards in the other.

On the opposite side of the lodge, my parents, aunts, and uncles tried to remain incognito but were doubled over in laughter.

Dannie and I looked at each other, our smiles widening.

Careening down Mattress Mountain came Kevin, his eyes narrow, his body compact. He held two poles, and strapped to his feet were a pair of downhill snow skis from the equipment shed. He flew down the mattresses and used his poles to keep himself upright until he hit the third-to-last mattress, lost all control, and flipped forward, his skis flying. Mom shrieked and began to laugh again as Kevin, in a heap at the bottom of the mountain, raised one pole to signal he was okay. A cheer erupted and the Feathers held up their boards marked with numbers to score his run. A solid 8.5.

As Kevin hobbled back up the path, Tommy and Mikey came racing down the mattresses in an oversized sled. Their eyes were wide as saucers, and both screamed at the top of their lungs with joy. Just as they flew off the track and launched the sled directly into the woods, Grannie and Gramps burst through the back screen door of the lodge.

Gramps's face was already working, sure that someone needed heavy discipline.

"What in God's goddamn name is going on out here?"

Grannie only looked fearful. "I heard screaming from inside. Who's hurt?"

They stopped in their tracks as they came upon Angie speeding down Mattress Mountain on a pair of roller-skates. Her hair flew behind her maniacally and she hollered in euphoria.

Grannie sucked in hard as Angie lost balance and landed in a painful version of the splits.

"What in the hell?!" Gramps yelled.

The cousins ignored Gramps and began to cheer and laugh while holding up their scores. 9.5.

Angie shook her fist in champion form and hobbled off the pathway to make room for the next contestant.

Grannie gently pulled at Gramps's arm and beckoned him back inside. Gramps scowled once more at the scene but surrendered with a grunt. "I better see every single goddamn item put away when this nonsense is through." I couldn't be sure, but I thought I caught a smirk on his face as he left his family to its comradery.

The contestants made their way steadily down the track, and each run ended in triumphant injury and delightful hysteria.

And as Dannie and I raced up the path to jump in line, I looked back at my parents. Dad had his arms around Mom, and they swayed together in laughter. Tammy and Richard high-fived each other with elation, while Patty held a cold beer in her hand, reveling in the festiveness. My body warmed. I knew to hold onto this moment, to take this mental picture. Of my parents happy and together. Of our family, safe and secure.

After the final votes were cast and winners declared, we marched like ants, climbing the blue stone path, mattresses hoisted above our heads in a single line back to the bunk beds. They were stained by grass and covered in dirt and sand, but no one paid any mind. We felt only amusement while recounting the myriad topples and pratfalls taken that afternoon.

Dannie and I reached the girls bunk first and opened the door. The smell was more noxious than I'd imagined.

"Oh man," I gagged.

"I know."

"Is it the cheese? I didn't know it could smell like that."

Dannie rolled her eyes. "It's totally grody. Help me open the windows."

"I don't think it's helping." I said holding one hand over my nose and waving the other around in the breezeless room.

"Tell me about it." Dannie froze, staring out the window. I walked up beside her and saw Amy sashaying down the path, the figure in front of her just out of my line of sight. Dannie's eyes narrowed.

"What's wrong?"

Dannie shook her head slowly as she walked silently into the bathroom and closed the door behind her.

I stayed at the window and watched Amy. Her hair bounced behind her, accentuating every step. She was even more tanned than when she arrived, and her caramel skin glistened under the slathering of baby oil. A wave of energy surged through me as my eyes lingered on her legs and arms. Her neck. Her collarbone. I knew those places now. Knew them well. Intimately. I had never been possessive of anyone before, but I felt with no uncertainty that Amy belonged to me. Not as an object, but as a soul that had shared my largest moment. We were connected. I bore my gaze into her and waited for her to feel that connection, to turn to me.

For a split second I had an image of Amy running to me and jumping up, her legs straddling my waist, her body engulfing mine. But she continued on, out of my sight and out of my reach.

Chapter 16

W hen Dannie finally arrived for dinner, I was already halfway through our annual red beans and rice. I shoveled in the mixture, nodded politely whenever Grannie or Gramps tried to include me in their conversations, and tried desperately not to laugh when Aunt Genevieve belched. I motioned to Dannie to come sit with me, sending her a telepathic message for help. She smiled, grabbed a bowl of beans, and joined our table.

That night we were with the elders and Tommy's parents, Kelly and Mark. Dannie wavered slightly as she slid into her seat, and it seemed to take a moment for her eyes to focus on her spoon. I watched her slowly slip her spoon into the bowl, scoop out a small portion, and carefully place it in her mouth. It was like watching a robot imitating a human's motions. Gramps eyed her silently.

"So, basically, this market is a gold mine right now," Mark said. "And the value of my seat on the CBOT is off the charts." Mark leaned back in his seat, his hands clasped behind his head in satisfaction. Kelly beamed.

Genevieve poured herself another glass of wine and hiccupped. Dannie began to giggle. I bit my lip as Gramps shot her a warning glance, which missed its mark.

"I'm going to say it again. I think it would be a wise move to let me handle some of your savings. This market is foolproof."

Gramps grunted. "Nothing is foolproof, and the fact that you think something is proves just how ignorant of the world you still are."

Kelly smiled sweetly. "Charles, it's just that this is such a good time to take advantage of the economy. Most of the husbands of my Junior League girls work with Mark. They are all doing incredibly well."

"She's right, Gramps." Mark patted Kelly's hand.

I watched as Dannie wavered with each bite. Grannie watched Gramps, measuring his mood, and Genevieve continued with her beans. There was a feeling of imbalance, like the sensibility at the table was about to topple on its side at any moment.

Gramps set his fork down a little too hard and bore into Mark. "I'll tell you what to take advantage of. Hard work. Skill. Productivity. Not standing in a large room, screaming at the top of your lungs about some invisible currency called *stocks* that you've made up. You can't count on that. One day it's high and you're rich as God, the next you're living in a box on the street. You don't have that when you really work."

"Gramps, I work every day."

"Not like what I'm talking about. I survived the war. I came to America. I built this business from nothing. I went into an office every day, went out with a toolbox every single goddamn day, and came home with dirty hands every night. I hired people. I gave them tools. I taught them skills. That's real work. That's something to be proud of." He picked his fork up again and gestured to Mark. "And let me tell you, I know exactly where my money stands. There are no surprises there for me. Not like with you. You know why? Because it's made with my hands. Not by waving a ticket in the air."

Gramps scooped up a bite of rice and turned to Kelly. "And *you* would do better to use your time not being a lady who lunches or spends her day at the spa. Instead, you should use your time teaching that boy of yours to put on some clothes." As if on cue, Tommy streaked through the dining hall with Mikey on his heels. Gramps raised an eyebrow. "At least for dinner."

Grannie patted Gramps's hand as Kelly fought back indignant tears. Mark surrendered his hands in the air. "All right, all right. I know when to say when." He leaned over and whispered to Kelly. "It's okay."

"Actually, it's not." Gramps leveled his gaze again.

"Charles." Grannie's patience waned.

"No. This is my place to say what I like. I am head of this house, am I not?" His accent grew thicker with his frustration. Grannie gave in, sighed heavily, and shook her head.

"This is what I am going to tell you both." Kelly and Mark sat like frightened students, their eyes wide and backs straight. "This is your time to work. You live your life behind a mask of ease and pleasure, and I am at a complete loss as to why this is a wonderful thing."

To Mark: "What legacy are you leaving?"

To Kelly: "What are you teaching your son?"

Gramps sat back, his fists on the table. "Kelly, how many days a week do you go out to lunch?" She stumbled for an answer. "Right. And how many nights do you cook a full meal for your family?"

"Well, we go out a lot. See, that's one of the perks—"

"A perk is showing your son you don't care enough to prepare his meals? That it is not important to sit in your home together and share your day without distraction?"

Mark broke in. "That's not fair, Gramps. I work hard so she can—"

"And you. Do you come straight home after the trade closes? I doubt it. Drinks after work with friends and co-workers? Easier to meet Kelly downtown for dinner rather than take the train home and turn around to come back into the city?" Gramps was gathering speed and we all sat in eager anticipation of what he would unleash next. "And I will also guess that it's easier to leave Tommy at home with a sitter rather than drag him downtown late at night. Especially if you can't keep him dressed!"

"Charles, quit being a bully." Genevieve slurred. Grannie caught my eye and gave a wary smile.

"He's always been a bully," Genevieve said.

Gramps regarded Genevieve and sighed as the remainder of his energy dissolved. Slowly, he lifted his face. "I just worry. Rose and I have worked hard. Both of us. We have worked to pay for our family, we have worked to create our family, worked to raise our family. And that takes time. It takes effort. It takes selflessness." He paused and looked softly at Dannie. "It takes putting others first. Knowing what's truly important in your life." Then back to Mark and Kelly. "I think maybe I have just heard too much talk today of lofty plans."

Mark glanced at Dannie, who seemed deaf to the whole conversation. "Ron talked to you about investing?"

Gramps shushed him with his hand. "Yes. And it scares me." He paused. "I am proud of my family because we built it ourselves and it's solid. Not because it was all fun and games and we made it look good. I want you to feel that same pride when you're my age."

Mark nodded. He knew Gramps well. His bark was loud, but his bite was filled with love. Kelly, still unable to warm herself to Gramps, sat back pouting. The atmosphere around the table felt as suffocating as the air outside. I was an anxious rabbit ready to bolt. All the talk of building a family, of raising a family, of the future had lit my fears on fire like crackling fireworks.

A roar of laughter rose from the Feathers's table. At that moment, I wished more than anything to be sitting with them.

Genevieve reached for the wine bottle. As she did, a guttural belch erupted. The alcohol and beans were a lethal mix in her aging body.

Grannie gasped. "Gennie. My word." Dannie started to giggle. Bits of rice fell from her mouth as her face darkened red with uncontrollable belly laughs. She tried to rein in, bobbing in her seat as tears welled up in her eyes. I threw dagger glances at her. Grannie shook her head disapprovingly at the whole scene.

"Cut it out, Dannie," Kelly grumbled. You're being disrespectful."

Gramps snapped her. "You leave her be."

Dannie's irrepressible giggles continued, and she gasped for air while trying to keep from spitting food across the table. She smacked a hand over her face to muffle herself, with no success.

Gramps turned to me, slightly put off. "Take her into the kitchen. Give her three aspirin and a full glass of water. Then take her up to her cabin and put her to bed."

"Yes sir." I rose and yanked Dannie out of her chair, thankful for a reason to leave.

Once in the kitchen, I let the faucet run until the water became ice cold, then filled her glass and handed her the aspirin. "What's up with you?"

She downed the pills and shrugged listlessly. "What's up with *you*?"

"What do you mean what's—"

From outside the kitchen's back door, a high-pitched scream pierced the air. It was followed by a second scream from a different, higher voice.

The door flew open and Ron tumbled in, gasping for air as he quickly zipped up his pants. "Jesus Christ! *Jesus Christ!*"

Eric and Angie walked into the kitchen to clear their plates. "Whoa. What happened?"

"That fucking bear tried to attack us!"

Family members started to trickle in, half done with dinner, half drawn by the shouting.

"You and who?"

Ron paused for only a split second, but it was enough to spur a quick glance between Eric and Angie.

"Me. I meant it tried to attack me."

"What is the yelling about?" Gramps came into the kitchen with a league of family in tow. He stood in front of Ron as if squaring off, his army behind him.

"That fucking bear!"

"Watch your goddamn language." Gramps glared at Ron. "What bear? Old Papa?"

"What other bear is there?"

The snickers started slowly and quietly, coming from the back and moving through the growing crowd like a wave. I couldn't help myself. A smile tugged at the corners of my mouth. Like all of us at one point or another, Ron had simply been startled by Old Papa.

"You think this is funny?" Ron turned beet red and spittle flew from his mouth.

Gramps raised his hand, gesturing for Ron to calm down. "What happened?"

"I was standing out back—"

"With your pants down." Angie quipped. Eric shook his head.

Ron threw a menacing glance. "He came up right behind me. I stepped backwards and then he stood up."

"And?" Patty had been silently watching the scene from the side of the kitchen. Her tone lacked sympathy, as did the look on her face. It was no longer about the bear. Ron, himself, was being questioned.

"*And*…I didn't want to stick around to see what he was going to do next," Ron said sarcastically. "That's when I ran in here."

"Who else was out there?" The emotional void in Patty's voice was unsettling.

Ron set his shoulders and his eyes fixed on Patty's. "Nobody."

Dannie grabbed the back of my shirt. Both of us had been here and we knew he was lying. She needed my voice.

"I heard two screams." The words felt foreign coming from my mouth. Ron's steely gaze rolled over to me. My knees buckled. All the air had been sucked out of the room. The laughter died quickly, and Ron shifted his weight uncomfortably. Patty stood stone still with Mom on one side and Tammy on the other.

"That's not the point," Ron said, trying to muster his previous energy. "Old Papa isn't a pet. He's a wild animal. That could have been a little kid out there instead of me. What then? Huh? What if it had been Tommy?" Then to my mother, "Or Mikey."

Mom's expression never changed.

"Would it have been so funny then?" He looked around the room and found no sympathy. No laughter. Nothing. His jury had reached its decision.

"Somebody needs to do something about it!"

Dannie burst out from behind me. "Old Papa is not an *it*! *He* belongs here!"

Gramps turned to me. "I told you to put her to bed."

"Yes, sir." Relieved by the reprieve, I grabbed Dannie's hand and led her away from Ron, from the family, from the tension. Behind me, I could hear the scene continue, the comments threading into one another.

"Ron, calm down!" Patty snapped.

"I won't calm down! Why are we waiting for a tragedy before doing something about that thing?"

"Nothing is going to happen."

"He's been sniffing around here forever."

"You're just embarrassed."

"The hell I am! I'm going to kill that fucking bear!"

"You're being a pussy."

"Eric! Language."

"Sorry, Grannie. But he is. You want to hit me, big man?"

"I'd like to see how you react to a bear attack!"

"Ron, back off." Patty was clearly finished with the conversation.

"He didn't attack you. He walked up and scared you," Tammy said evenly.

"Yeah, and you still haven't answered what you were doing? Or who you were doing it with."

"Not now, Angie."

"I'm sorry, Patty. I just think he's full of bullshit and you don't deserve that."

"Angie." Mom was also growing weary of the situation.

"It's true. And everyone knows it."

"You think just because you grew up with money, your little prep school, your Ivy League college sorority, you think you're better than me?"

"No, I think I'm better than you because I am better than you, asshole."

"Eric, take Angie outside, please."

"You got it, Gramps."

"I'm gonna kill that fucking bear, I swear!"

"Shut up, Ron."

The screen door slammed, and I could hear Eric and Angie not far behind us.

"He's such a dick!"

"I know, but you can't spout off like that. It's not cool."

Angie sighed heavily. "I know. I just feel so bad for Patty. And Dannie. They deserve so much better." Their voices faded as they walked down toward the bonfire, undoubtedly ready to relive every moment with the rest of the Feathers who had missed the action.

I turned to Dannie, but she stared straight ahead as if Angie wasn't even there. As if I wasn't there. I finally understood this new behavior of hers. It was her defense; it was her own mind trick for coping. She looked absent because she *was* absent.

She was trying to survive.

I held her hand and guided her the rest of the way to the girls' cabin. Thankfully, we found it empty, and I left the lights off, hoping to keep Dannie in a calm state.

The moment we stepped inside, she stopped in her tracks. My body was ready to jump in case she decided to run off.

"Gag. It still smells in here." The disgust in Danny's voice was completely valid in the lingering stench.

I turned. She was looking right at me, smiling sadly.

I nodded and smiled back. "Totally. For sure." I opened a window while Dannie crawled into bed fully clothed. I looked down at her, the threadbare blanket pulled up to her chin. It was too hot to be wrapped in anything, but I didn't try to take it from her. That night it wasn't a blanket. It was armor. That Ron had been up to his womanizing ways again was obvious. With whom, I couldn't quite figure out. The obvious answers were either Rena, who loved Eric so deeply it seemed an impossibility, or Tabitha, who in her constant disheveled state seemed the more likely culprit.

"What was up with you tonight?" I asked.

Dannie peered at me mischievously, "I might have found some of the Feathers's wine coolers this afternoon."

My eyebrows rose. "How many did you find?"

"Maybe a four-pack?" I rolled my eyes.

"Maybe two four-packs?"

"What?" My jaw dropped.

"Ughhh. But I don't feel so awesome now." She rolled onto her side.

"Well, don't throw up and choke on your vomit," I joked.

As I turned to walk away, a conversation outside the window stopped me. I looked out but it was pitch black. It didn't matter; the voices were clear as bells.

"You dickhead. You left me to die."

"You weren't going to die. He just wanted the trash."

"Oh really? Is that why you screamed like a girl and ran inside?"

"You screamed too."

"I have a right to scream. *I am* a girl."

"No." The voice lowered slightly. "You're no girl."

Giggle.

"No girl I know can do what you can do. You're a woman."

"So, you liked that, huh?"

"Oh yeah."

"You're lucky I didn't bite your dick off. I was scared shitless!"

"Hey, I wouldn't let anything happen to you."

"Liar. You were totally out of there."

"Okay, okay. Let me make it up to you."

Pause.

"How?"

"How do you want me to make it up to you?"

Silence.

"That's what I thought."

Silence. Moan.

"Come on. I know a place. No people. And no bears."

Giggle.

Footsteps.

My heart felt like it might beat out of my chest as it shattered at the brazenness of Ron's traitorous actions. I turned to walk away when Dannie's hand shot out and grabbed mine. I had forgotten she was there.

She had heard it, too.

Her face was stone, but tears poured over her nose, over her cheek, onto her pillow. She gently pulled me down until I was lying next to her and my arm was wrapped over her body. She held on tightly as I cradled her.

Another layer of armor.

Chapter 17

I t was dusk, and the weathered pontoon showed its age.
The cream-colored pleather seats, dingy and spotted
yellow, were dried out, cracked after years of enduring
weight and weather. The turquoise carpeting that covered
the floor was matted, with gray sunspots and dingy brown
frayed edges. The steering wheel was covered in a hundred
layers of sticky substances, all congealed to create a slick,
hard-shell crust. The smell wafting up from the boat itself
told a history of lake water, wet molded towels, and spilled
cocktails. No one noticed, though. All we saw was a vessel
of familial love.

The pontoon sagged under the weight of so many people.
We had no concept of max capacity. Our only concern being
the accommodation of every person who wanted to go,
could be coerced, or had been playfully forced to join. The
more the merrier in our clan.

The Feathers crammed in together, piled on laps on laps
on top of laps. Angie squealed with delight. Her braces
glistened and filled out her mouth. Eric gave Paul a playful
shove and sent the row of cousins tumbling like dominos.
They let out protests and whoops as their contraband beer
sloshed over the sides of their red plastic Solo cups.

"Eric, you turd!"

"Angie, language."

"Sorry Grannie!" Angie hopped up, stumbled over legs
and feet, and threw her arms around Grannie in a bear hug.

Grannie's hair was not yet snow white but still peppered with her dark, rich Italian color. She shared the driver's seat with Gramps who, like a pilot, went through his boat captain's checklist before the nightly pontoon cocktail cruise. He flipped lights on and off, moved the rudder right and left.

My mother and father sat side by side, sipping their gin and tonics while comfortably conversing with Tammy and Richard. Mom's body was full and healthy, her cheeks flushed with laughter and gin. Ann and Kate sat up front with Tony and Burt, already a few drinks ahead of everyone else as they reminisced about the good old times.

I sat on the back platform, my legs stretched out before me, entwined with Dannie's. She sat opposite me, her hair cropped to her shoulders, her teeth gapped and crooked. Her nose was burnt and peeled three layers deep, her thick-strapped swim team swimsuit peeked out from her tank top. She smiled and grabbed my feet as anchors as she swayed and pretended to throw us off the boat.

"Hey," I shouted at her as her laughter rose.

"Scaredy," she shouted back, bringing her heel down on my shin. I reeled back and forth dramatically, howled at the sky, and rolled my eyes back in my head while cradling my leg. Dannie fell to her side and hung half off the back of the pontoon and giggled at my spectacle. The boat engine started up with a loud whir then settled into a low, steady purr. We jerked backward then forward as Gramps set out on the lake.

Behind the sounds of our family's conversation was a peaceful drone of cicadas, evening bird songs, and the calling loon. On the shore, I saw the lightning bugs come out and magically illuminate the beach. The lake itself was still, and the setting sun cast a deep pink and orange film over everything, like we were watching the scene through a sepia camera lens.

The conversation quieted and the family nestled into one another as dusk quickly fell around us. I looked around at the tranquility that connected every person. Grannie lay her head on Gramps's shoulder, his reciprocation a gentle kiss on the top of her head.

Mom was tucked into Dad's neck, while Tammy and Richard held each other serenely. The rest of the cousins furthered their entanglement. Like crawling ivy, they weaved in and out of one another with no beginning or end.

Dannie scooted over on her bottom and, without hesitation or thought, took my hand. We watched a loon behind the boat dive and emerge, trying to guess where it would pop up next.

We motored in silence around the lake, peace infused into all of us. We were warm with kinship. We were full of love. We were cloaked in the safety of our family.

As the sun dipped behind the Jack Pines, Gramps lifted his red Solo cup and began the Polish drinking song we all knew by heart.

"Pi-je kuba do ja-ku-ba,
Ja-kub do Mi-cha-ta."

Gramps barely got through the first line before everyone lifted their glasses and joined in.

"Pi-jesz-ty, pi-je korn-pa-ni-ja cata.
A kto-nie wy-pi-je,
Te-go we dwa ki-je"

And then at the top of our lungs,

"Tu- pu cu-pu, cu-pu tu-pu, te-go we dwa ki-je!"

We continued along the lake and finished the verses, swaying back and forth to the folk tune while the adults sipped from their cups and passed around cheers.

I was engulfed by the sound of laughter, the feeling of love, and the safety of Dannie's hand.

But something was wrong. I could feel it. Frantically looking around, I realized my mother was missing. Then a figure, standing alone on the dock behind us, caught my eye. My mother stood, solitary, waving goodbye. That couldn't be right, though. She had just been sitting next to my father. Panic rose in my throat and I opened my mouth to scream but no noise came out. I screamed and screamed for Gramps to turn around. We had left my mother! But no one could hear me as they continued to sing, hugging and smiling, completely unaware we were floating further and further away from the dock.

ॐ

I OPENED MY eyes, unsure of where I was. I glanced over at the other beds. Arms were flung over sides and feet stuck out from under sheets. Dawn had just broken through the windows.

I rolled back over and squeezed my body as close as I could to the wall before squeezing my eyes shut and praying to fall back into my dream. I prayed my mother would be back on the boat. I prayed someone else would notice and return to pick her up.

I knew my prayers were falling on deaf ears.

I pulled the thin plaid blanket up over my head, creating a cocoon to hide my tears. My mother was on a dock out of reach, and we were all floating farther from her. The reality of time crushed down around me. While I'd been aware the inevitable would come, there'd been the sense that *inevitable* was far in the future. With heavy tears streaming down my face, I knew the truth was only around the corner. I'd taken so much for granted, both in the past and about what lay ahead.

I saw images of Mom delicately lifting waffles out of the iron, slathering them with butter and syrup, while we gleefully gorged ourselves without a *thank you*. Swiftly scribbling a meaningless message on a birthday card for her, viewing it as a chore rather than a moment to express my love. Silently cursing her in my head when forced to spend time with the family instead of attending a sleepover. Rolling my eyes when she would come in to kiss me goodnight. Every night.

There would come a moment, I realized, when she would no longer tiptoe in to kiss the top of my head. There would be no more birthday cards. No more peaceful Sunday mornings with the smell of waffles in the air. I would miss so much of what she'd done in the past, and she would miss so much of what I'd do in my future.

She would never take photos of my prom. I would never go on a college campus tour with her. She would never know me as a new eighteen-year-old voter, as a twenty-one-year-old ordering my first legal drink. I'd never even had a girlfriend, and yet I mourned that she would never meet my future bride. Would never hold her grandchild. Her blood would be a part of the baby's being, yet her fingers would never have a chance to caress the tiny toes. My heart sank at the futility of it all.

I shoved it all inward. The guilt, the fear, the worry, the pain. I shoved down the knowledge of fate and of impending doom. I crumpled it all like a piece of paper, smaller and smaller until it was little more than a pinpoint of black in my core. I ignored the demon that is time, circling us like a hungry wolf.

Still, I couldn't block it all out. One image held fast.

And as my mother looked on from the dock, the boat slowly moving on without her, all I could do was wave goodbye.

Chapter 18

I sat on the edge of the dock, my toes dangling and dipping into the lake. The hot wood under my thighs seared my legs, but I barely felt it. My mind was hazy, like it had used all the power it could muster.

The camp was quiet. The heat, unbelievably, had intensified to the point of causing ripples in the horizon. Nearly everyone had scrambled to the Duluth shopping mall in search of air conditioning.

I heard a familiar shuffle coming for me. I didn't need to turn around to know it was Dad.

"Ready to go, sport?"

I hoped my slumped shoulders would be attributed to the heat. I pulled myself up slowly and forced a smile.

"Bring on the bluegill." I took the fishing poles from Dad while he loaded a cooler and the bait into the Alumacraft.

The lake was empty, save for a pair of loons. I watched, hypnotized as they drifted and dove and cried their melancholy song. The boat puttered along until we reached our favorite nook. Every year it was thick with fish, and we kept it a secret, our special destination.

Dad turned off the motor and, for a moment, we were swallowed by the sudden silence and stillness of Black Bear Lake. I looked over the side of the boat and saw the bluegill slowly circle and pause, then circle again, back and forth. Without a word, I pulled a worm from my bait container, a small white cardboard box that could have easily been mistaken for Chinese take-out. I threaded the hook through the worm and gently dipped my rod backward, then straight ahead as the release of my thumb sent the line out, hissing into the middle of the weed beds. I waited a few minutes, then slowly turned the handle, winding the line back in, then tilting the rod and starting the process over. The repetition calmed me, and I found my mind release and my stomach unclench with every cast.

We sat for a half-hour, our backs peacefully to each other, without a single bite. I turned to my father and realized he wasn't casting his line. He wasn't threading bait or even holding his pole. His shoulders were straight, but his brow was furrowed as he stared off into nothingness.

"Dad?"

He blinked once, then twice, as if waking, and turned to me with an expression like he had forgotten I was there. He looked at me—looked through me—with moist eyes. He smiled sadly while exhaling.

"Sorry. I suppose I'm not the best fishing partner today."

"It's okay." But it wasn't okay. I had so many questions, and more than ever I needed some real answers. I wanted some direction, some sort of light in all the darkness that surrounded my world. I needed someone to know what was happening.

We floated in silence for a minute more, then Dad turned to face me.

"I think—I believe—that if I could go back, I'd do many things differently." He looked off in the distance; he wasn't speaking to me. "Your mother and I came from such different families. And it was very difficult for us both. But especially for her."

He swallowed hard. "She came from"—he paused and limply gestured towards the camp—"all of this. And not just the money. I mean, the actual family. Our backgrounds, our base, our foundation…we were built from different materials, cut from very different cloths. Her family is loud, a nonstop party. Shouted opinions and fiery arguments. It was so new and scary to me when we dated. Completely unchartered territory." His brow furrowed again. "All I could think to do was tighten my own house. Create my own family in the image I was comfortable with. Quiet, logical, like living in a library and not a home."

I thought of his parents, themselves professors. My most vivid picture of them was sitting in front of the fireplace in their Arts and Crafts home, books in their laps and Tiffany lamps lighting the corners of the room. Quiet as a church, voices barely louder than whispers. I always loved visiting them and their safe, comforting demeanor.

Dad turned to me. "You know, our house is very similar to my own childhood home." He smiled to himself. "I'm realizing now that I even made sure things were placed in the same drawers as they were when I was growing up. Dishes to the right of the stove, socks in the second drawer down." He chuckled. "It's funny. I always thought of your grandfather as being so controlling, but in my own passive way, I was just as bad."

The smile left his face. "And your mother handled all of that control with such grace and dignity." He sat in silence for a moment, lost in thought, eyes on the shoreline. "And she didn't need to be controlled. Not her. That's the ironic thing about it all. You might not know it, but she is a very strong woman. A very opinionated woman. But she never fought your grandfather and she never fought me. I think her greatest strength was knowing that her father and her husband both needed to feel in control to feel safe. She provided that for us both." He paused and his eyes grew moist again. "She's given so much."

I sat in silence. My soul was overwhelmed. Drowning. I was trying to swim but kept sinking and, as much as I wanted to reach out, to ask questions, to make a comment, to agree or disagree, my lips remained unmoving.

I glanced up at Dad's profile. I had never seen him cry before. Even when we first learned about Mom's illness, he was stoic, the family rock. He motored forward with a *life must go on* mentality. He held his head high as was his nature, never betraying his true fears and pain. To see a crack in him shook me to the core.

He continued. "Your mother is very sick."

"I know." The words would barely come out.

His lip quivered. "No. She's very sick, Adam. It's worse. We had some hope at one point, but now…"

A bluegill swam in circles as it protected its eggs, which were hidden in the weeds, translucent and vulnerable. I stared at it without seeing it. I had known my mother was ill—was very ill—and I had known she would pass away. But I didn't want to hear it. To hear it made it real, and I didn't want it to be real. The anxiety and fear of the unknown had lingered over us for so long, I didn't know how I would feel when it was time to move on. I didn't want to know.

I wanted my mom.

We spent the rest of the afternoon in silence, floating above the nesting beds, our rods at our feet.

The bluegill continued keeping vigil.

Chapter 19

T he adults stayed in the lodge after dinner, embroiled in a deep and heavy discussion. Gramps had met with lawyers to set up a trust that would pay for the camp long after he passed away. A portion of his current savings would be needed to establish the fund. The adults were split in two camps: those who wanted the compound at Black Bear Lake, and those who just wanted their inheritance. Ron was vocal about his wishes, and the room grew tense. Tammy finally erupted, pointing out that any inheritance was Patty's and not his. The heated debate had just turned ugly when the kids decided to sneak out the back door.

We gathered on the porch that overlooked the lake. Angie rifled through a pile of cassette tapes until she found John Cougar, then cranked the music as high as the boombox's volume would go. Paul grabbed Angie's hand and whirled her in a circle as she squealed with delight. Contagious laughter swirled around the cousins. We rhythmically bumped hips, wiggled, gyrated, throwing our bodies left to right in an ecstatic frenzy as we sang about Jack & Diane at the top of our lungs.

I took Dannie's hand. She grinned at me, and we began to spin. I grabbed both her wrists and we circled round and round, bumping into cousins before we switched dance partners and laughed until joyous tears streamed down our faces.

It was my dream all over again, the warmth and comfort of my family. We were secure together. Safe. And, above all, we were happy. It was a remarkable happiness, I realized, that came only from them.

Later, as we sat around the fire pit, Eric played an acoustic rendition of John Denver's *Rocky Mountain High*, and I lost myself in the flickering flames. Dannie talked one of the cousins out of a Leinenkugel and she slowly sipped on it, the condensation dripping off the bottle and down her hand. Angie gazed at us through tipsy, watery eyes.

"I remember when we used to babysit you guys up here. When you were, like, five."

She reminisced with a sentimental smile. Paul leaned over, wrapped his arm around her and gently kissed her on the forehead.

I felt what Angie felt, the love that would come from being no place but right here with each other. We were a safety net, whether we were aware of it or not. We might fall from great heights, slip off the tightropes we constantly walked, but below us, always, we had each other to cushion the landing.

Dannie took another sip and rested her head on my shoulder. I leaned back against her, and the rest of the world fell away.

I was almost lulled to sleep by the setting when, from the top of the walkway, up the hill by the cabins, we heard screams.

Eric and Paul jumped up, ready for heroism, when Tommy appeared and streaked by with his hair flying behind him.

"Buuuuuuuuuuuuuuugs!" He screamed and made a beeline for the lodge. He moved too fast to keep himself from hitting the screen door. It didn't slow him down. He ripped through the mesh and kept going.

Amused, I turned to Dannie. "Bugs?"

The look on her face stopped my laughter cold.

She glanced up at then cabins and then at me. "You can't be mad at me. It's just a prank."

"Oh, man," I moaned and ran to the boys' cabin.

"You said I couldn't be mad at you about the cheese. It's the same thing." Dannie said as she ran after me. "You can't be mad at me!"

The scene at the cabin was complete chaos.

The boys ran around the cabin, screaming and swatting at the air with blankets and pillows, smacking each other's backs and arms in defense.

"Shit!" I screamed when I saw what had happened. I yelled again at Dannie when she caught up to me, peered inside the cabin and, despite the remorseful look in her eyes, began to laugh.

The insects resembled a low-hanging black cloud. Mosquitos, gnats, no-see-ums, mayflies and biting flies all dodged right and left, up and down, escaping attempts to smash or clear them out. The bugs dove and weaved and bombed the boys' faces, arms, and legs. Between screeches of surprise and the flinging of pillows against the walls and ceiling, every cousin was scratching exposed skin. Kevin saw me through the window and ran outside.

"Dude! Somebody left the door wide open and all the lights on. It attracted every bug on this lake. I swear, I'm gonna kill Tommy and Mikey!"

"It wasn't Tommy or Mikey."

"They're the only dipshits dumb enough to leave all the lights on and the door—" He stopped when he realized I was staring at Dannie, who had quickly backtracked down to the bonfire, her laughter audible though the woods. "A prank? This was a prank?!"

"Yup. And I see the back windows are missing screens, too." We walked around the side of the cabin and found them leaning against the wall.

Kevin turned to me. "What do we do?"

I shrugged my shoulders, smirked in appreciation of the girls' ingenious plan, and snapped the screens back into place.

"Let's go kill some bugs."

Chapter 20

Dannie and I sneered at each other from either side of the net, both of us bent over, hands on our knees. She made a gesture like slitting her throat and I countered back by punching one hand into the palm of the other. She narrowed her eyebrows and I narrowed mine. She mouthed, *You're gonna die*, and I mouthed back, *You first*. She let loose a guttural growl, and just as I was ready to make my own dangerous animal noise, the volleyball smacked the back of my head, knocking me face-first into the sand.

Dannie fell over laughing and the shouts from my teammates began.

"Get up, you big baby!"

"Why didn't you hit the ball?"

"Jeez, that was the perfect set up for a spike, too."

"Nice job, douche!"

But I didn't mind. I stayed there on the ground for a minute, a slight smile on my face, and enjoyed the moment's rest. We had played the first round in the tournament, and the sun had come out early with a vengeance. The sand burned my bare back, but the smell of roasting pig numbed my other senses. It had been turning on the spit all morning and would continue until mid-afternoon, when it would be taken down and gently pulled for the evening's feast. The combination of smoky aroma and good-natured ribbing satiated me. I would have stayed there all day if a shadow hadn't fallen over my closed eyes.

"That's what I thought." I squinted up at Dannie's silhouette, hands on her hips as she stared down at me. Before she could move, I swung my leg, sweeping it against her ankles, knocking her backward off her feet and onto the sand next to me. She looked at me shocked, then smiled and punched me in the stomach.

"Come on, cuz," Angie said. "Let's get this game going!" She jumped up and down, swinging punches at the air. After a short recess to take a swig from their beer bottles, the other cousins returned to the volleyball court.

Dannie and I had just brushed the sand off each other's backs when Amy sauntered out from around the lodge. Her hair was tangled in the back, and she ran her fingers through it while straightening her shorts over bikini bottoms.

"Hey, nice of you to show up," Angie teased.

"Which side am I on?" Amy asked nonchalantly.

Dannie stared coldly. "Neither. We don't need you."

"I thought you needed a replacement for Eric." Amy paused for effect. "After you smashed the ball into his nose."

I took a step closer to Dannie. "Rena is taking his place."

Rena had not actually participated but instead stood on the sideline, drinking her beer. She threw her hands in the air. "I don't care. She can take my spot."

Angie rolled her eyes at Eric, who shrugged his shoulders as Rena threw her arms around him, squealing. Terry sighed and turned to Amy. "Listen, we started two hours ago. We're on a roll. I think it's best if we keep going as is."

Amy cocked her hip and tilted her head coyly. "Come on."

"We said we don't need you." The words came strong and hard out of my mouth.

Amy stiffened. "Cool." She turned, then swayed her hips as she walked toward the beach.

Dannie linked her pinkie with mine and whispered, "Thank you."

The game continued with the previous laughter, drinking and mockery between the cousins. But I knew, with the slight change in the shade of her eyes, the minute diminishment of her spark, that Amy had taken a sliver of Dannie with her.

Chapter 21

I sat lethargic on the beach with a handful of Minnows, scooping sand into small piles that they formed into mini forts connected by deep water canals. Listening to their chatter, I closed my eyes and fell back. Shrieking, the kids swooped in and began to cover my body with scoopful after scoopful of hot sand.

"Adam. Adam!" My mother was yelling from the shore. Much to the Minnows's chagrin, I sat up.

"Adam, a canoe broke free. Would you go fetch it?"

I let out an exasperated sigh. We had a continent's worth of relatives surrounding us. Why did I have to be continually singled out? Mom and I had been at odds all day, with an especially nasty exchange just hours before, leaving me raw, angry, and exhausted. I desperately needed to be left alone.

"Can't Kevin get it?"

"Adam!" Mom's incredulous voice answered my question. I stood slowly, brushing myself off and dragging my feet to the shoreline. The canoe was in the middle of the lake, and I felt fatigued just looking at how far I'd have to swim.

I stomped past her to the end of the pier. As I dove in the water, she yelled out again, but I stayed under and swam, drowning her out.

My muscles shook as I finally neared the canoe. I floated on my back, gasping for air, willing my calves not to cramp.

I was struck by the silence. For the first time since I'd arrived at Black Bear Lake, I was alone. And for a moment it was bliss. I grabbed the side of the canoe and floated for a moment, enjoying the peace.

When I finally tried to pull myself into the canoe, it flipped, crashing over my head. After several failed attempts, and one moment when I was certain of death, I wiggled my body into the boat. Panting, I laid on the floor, sprawled, every muscle quivering from exhaustion. Slowly, the realization of my fatal mistake drifted into my mind.

I had not brought an oar.

With a resigned sense of surrender, I moaned. I was considering waiting in the boat until it eventually floated to the other side of the lake when I heard a steady swish of water. I raised my head just high enough to peer over the edge of the canoe.

Ron was swimming toward me, breaking through the water with a strong stroke by his right arm while his left held an oar. He caught my eye for a moment and paused with a half-smile. I slid back down into the canoe, wishing Ron to simply evaporate into thin air. Staring into the sky, the oar appeared over my head. I reluctantly grabbed it and pulled it into the canoe. A few quiet seconds passed before Ron calmly called out. "Give me a hand, bud?"

Despite my great wish for him to drown, I exhaled dramatically and sat up. Treading water, Ron smiled at me. I stuck out my hand, expressionless.

"Sorry, bud, I think I'm too heavy for that. Just lean your body against the other side."

I moved across the canoe and thought *Don't call me bud.* I leaned hard as Ron pulled himself up and over the side. He sat, breathing hard for a moment before chuckling at my expense.

"I saw you take off without an oar. Thought it might be a heck of a long trip back without one."

I managed one short nod but kept my eyes on the tree line at the edge of the lake.

"Plus, it gave me a break from the chaos at the camp." He added with a laugh. But the laugh died off quickly at my cold glance.

We sat in silence for what seemed like hours. And in that silence, I raged. I imagined hitting Ron over the head with the oar. I imagined punching him repeatedly in the face. I imagined holding him underwater and watching him thrash and fight for air.

He startled me out of my retribution. "I guess we can get going back."

I sat in front of him as he grabbed the oar and propelled us forward at a snail's pace. With no paddle to help, I turned my back to Ron and kept my focus on the beach far ahead.

Ron broke the silence again. "I'm really sorry about your Ma."

It was an ice pick to my gut. Ron paused, then continued, "I lost my mother when I was younger. Not as young as you, but still young. Seventeen. Lung cancer. She was a smoker. And now so am I. I guess that makes me the dumbass." I stayed facing away but closed my eyes.

He went on. "She worked the casinos in Reno. A real hellhole. You ever been?"

I didn't respond but Ron didn't seem to notice.

"Yup, shit central there. That's why I left. As soon as she passed, I split. Went to California and took care of myself since."

He continued to row slowly. I prayed for a gust of wind to come and speed up our ride back to shore.

"You know, thinking back, I wish I had spent that last bit of time with her. But man, when it was happening, the future just seemed to go on forever. I knew she was dying. Fuck, I was pissed at her. I mean *pissed*, you know? I was mad that she had smoked and that she hadn't gone to the doctor in time. I was mad that she kept working in a place where, even when she wasn't smoking, she was breathing in other people's smoke. But I guess I was most pissed at her because I didn't want her to be gone. That's really all it was. I knew I was going to miss her and that screwed me up, man."

I fought my tears hard, but lost the battle. I kept facing forward so Ron wouldn't see.

"I guess what I learned though it all is that the future is really just a snippet and, fuck, it passes fast. You have to make the most of life *now,* while it's happening. Not wait for tomorrow. Because there won't always be a tomorrow."

He paused. "That's why I'm following my dream." After a moment he asked, "You still writing shit in that notebook?"

The strangest longing pulsed through me. I wanted Ron to hug me. I wanted to sit with my uncle and cry in his arms. He knew what my dirty secret was, what had been ripping my heart apart for a year. He knew my anger. My pain. My shame.

Ron was a jerk, a bully, a slimeball. He was also the only one who saw right through me. And I was grateful to finally be seen.

At the lodge, Dad was literally up to his elbows in grease as he moved methodically from one side of the pig to the other, pulling off long strands of tender meat. A nearby cattle farmer had slaughtered the swine. Other than that, the men oversaw all other aspects of the pig roast every year. They manned the spit and roaster for hours and poured fat droplets over the carcass as it turned. They made sheet pans full of gooey barbecue beans, glazed over with sticky, blackened molasses. Pallets of buns were bought from a local Amish bakery. The rolls were fresh, soft, and wonderfully, fragrantly yeasty. The three-bean salad was unjarred and poured into large serving bowls, the sharp smell of vinegar attacking my nose when I'd lean in too close. The cornbread was cut into generously large rectangles, with one thin layer of fatty bacon rendering applied to the top crust so it melted into the bread while it was still hot. The cobs of corn sat on the grill, turned over in short intervals, popping audibly. And row after row of butter, approximately one stick per person, sat on the counter, softening.

The long folding tables were covered with huge red- and white-checkered plastic tablecloths. Paper plates, napkins and plastic forks sat next to pitchers of sun tea and pink lemonade. At the end of the spread, on the ground, was a large metal washing basin filled with bottles of Leinenkugel covered in ice.

I hovered next to Dad and picked at pieces of stray pork right from the bone. Occasionally, he would pop an extra-tender piece in my mouth.

As the heady, dense smoke filled the air around me, my mind drifted to the sharp conversation Mom and I had earlier. It had left an ugly aftertaste in my mouth that was magnified by my encounter with Ron. A knot had been twisting in my stomach since the morning fight, a nagging mixture of guilt and frustration. It was the only time I could remember her allowing rage at her own body to come screaming forward.

"Why can't Kevin do it?"

"Adam..."

"I'm ALWAYS the one who fills the woodpile."

"You're older and stronger."

"He's not a baby!"

"Adam, please. I don't have the energy for this right now."

"Yeah, I know. You never have energy for anything anymore."

"What's that supposed to mean?"

"It's just that I'm like this family's servant."

"I need your help right now. Please don't fight me on this."

"No shit. Like I don't know that?"

"Adam!"

"Everyone needs my help. It's like I'm the only one who is capable of handling anything."

"I'm sorry you've had so much put on your plate, and I know you're frustrated, but—"

"No, you're not. You're not sorry."

"Why would you say that?"

"Because you don't care. All I hear anymore is 'Adam, get me this. Adam, get me that.'"

"I know it's hard to understand sweetheart, but I am simply unable to do what I used to."

"I know! You can't do ANYTHING! You can't even take care of your own kids anymore and I'm SICK of it!"

She paused, boiling.

Then, an explosion.

"Do you think I want this? You think I want to feel my muscles dying a little more every day? I can feel it, physically feel my body dying. Did you know that? Do you think I enjoy it?!"

Silence.

"Do you think I enjoy thinking about leaving you and your brothers? Leaving my husband? My family?"

More silence.

"Do you think I enjoy knowing this is it? The end of my future watching you grow, hugging you, holding you? You. My baby. How dare you tell me that I don't care! I care so much it hurts more than what I'm physically going through. My heart is broken!"

I realized I was shivering, thinking of Mom turning her back to me, sobbing. Thinking of my own paralysis at her words and fury, unable to move. Thinking of how she slowly walked away from me and my cruelty, how our only private conversation about her impending death had been so vicious.

Richard stuck his head out the kitchen's back door.

"John, the salad's chopped and ready. Do you have that dressing?"

Dad whistled slowly. "In a minute," he yelled back and turned to me. "Go run and find your mother. She should be up in the cabin. She was supposed to come down and show me how to make her salad dressing and I completely forgot."

Up at the cabin, I knocked quietly in case Mom was asleep. I glanced back over my shoulder at the surrounding woods. I could faintly hear shrieks of laughter from the beach, aunts yelling at their kids and boat motors starting up and shutting off. But up by the cabins, with the trees and leaves to soak up the noise, all was peaceful.

I knocked again, but Mom didn't come to the door. For a moment I panicked and ran into the cabin's bedroom, fearing that I'd find her cold and unconscious. But the cabin was empty. I breathed a deep sigh of relief.

"Mom?"

Nothing.

I put my head near the window and called out again, "Mom?"

No answer.

I walked back out onto the small porch and looked around. I called louder. The area by the cabins was empty, everyone below waiting for the feast. Mom hadn't been down with the family or out by the beach. I had come up the main blue stone pathway, so I knew I hadn't passed her as she came down. I decided to walk behind the cabins to where the woods began.

There was a game I'd played when I was younger. I was a Native American living in the woods, searching for animals to hunt for food, hiding from enemy tribes. I slithered up against trees, then slyly looked around to make sure no warriors were sneaking up on me. I crouched behind rocks and shrubs, waiting for an unsuspecting deer to come out of hiding and straight into my arrow's path.

I found myself again walking slowly, softly moving from one moss-covered stone to another, sidestepping crunchy dried leaves and loud, brittle sticks.

Then, movement ahead of me. Thinking it might be the fawn we had seen before, I stopped and bent down, crawling silently until I was behind a large white pine, then straightening up and peering around it.

In the center of a small, remote clearing stood my mother. Her face turned up to the sun, eyes closed. She looked miniature, her weight loss accentuating her already small frame. Mom's sweater lay on a log to the side and her T-shirt billowed like a ship's sail in the slight breeze. Her curls were piled up on her head and she glistened from the lotion liberally applied to her drying skin. She looked childlike. Peaceful.

For the first time ever, I truly saw her. Not as my mom. Not as Dad's wife. I saw *her*. All of her.

I saw the woman who at one time was a girl. I saw a girl who had run through fields with her friends, locking pinkies, swearing to be best friends forever. I saw her as a girl who defied her controlling father and ran away, only to return that evening in time for supper. I saw a girl who had her first kiss, a kiss that opened the world. I saw her as a person who grew physically and mentally. A person who had her first boyfriend, tried her first beer, her first cigarette, snuck out of her house for the first time. I saw her as a young woman with dreams, who stayed up late studying while her eyes drooped with fatigue. A young woman who made honor roll and gave her valedictorian speech with pride. A woman who entered the world, her soul full of hope and promise. I saw one dream get crushed, another shot down. I saw a woman who had fallen madly in love for the first time only to have her heart broken into a million pieces, pieces that never fully recovered. I saw a woman who slowly built a wall of protection around herself as the world lost its rosy hue. A person who tried and failed, tried and succeeded, tried and failed, and on and on.

I saw a woman who found a man that made her truly happy, a woman who found peace and contentment. A woman who finally saw a bright, secure, solid future. A woman who bore three children, found herself in them and lost herself because of them. A woman who had sacrificed with the best of intentions and had found joy in those sacrifices and fulfillment in the returns.

I saw a woman who cherished everything around her and would never wish to change her lot or her life. But I saw a woman who would, from time to time, look back.

A woman who was human. A woman who would think about the crushed dream, think about her broken heart. A woman who would not wish, but wonder, *What if?*

And as she looked up to the sun, with a hint of a smile on her face, I saw a woman who was no longer looking back, no longer looking forward. I saw a woman living in the now and feeling thankful for it.

As quietly as I approached, I retreated on the same soft, mossy stones and left her with her *now*.

Chapter 22

We floated on the pontoon for two hours, our bellies distended, filled with barbecued pork, beans, and cornbread. We resembled a pack of lions after a feast, our bodies draped over one another, barely able to move.

We filled red plastic cups with beer and gin and tonics, and we sang our favorite campfire songs between peaceful moments of silence and watching loons dip into the black water. Mom sat between Dad and me, and we wrapped our arms around her, blanketing her with our bodies. She gently kissed my forehead, and I was thankful for her forgiveness. Dannie sat on the other side of me, her legs thrown over mine as she leaned back into Aunt Patty's chest.

We pulled slowly into the dock, the light long gone in the sky. The family swayed silently while Grannie sang an old Italian love song.

The piercing gunshot came from nowhere, shattering our serenity.

"Was that a gun?" Richard asked as he darted to the side of the boat and grabbed a rope to pull us in.

"Go!" Gramps yelled over his shoulder to all of us. "I'll dock, just jump off and see what's going on."

We leapt from the pontoon and hit the dock running full force. Mom looked terrified. "John, the kids."

"I'm sure it's fine." But the tone in Dad's voice didn't sound sure and he sprinted up the dock.

We arrived at the beach and followed the Means and Minnows, who were also running toward the commotion. I rounded the corner of the lodge with Dannie right behind me and the Feathers closing in. I stopped cold in my tracks at the barbecue. The rest piled up behind me. We formed a widespread circle, as if no one would allow themselves to get any closer.

In the middle was the large grill, along with Ron, who held a shotgun, and Old Papa, who lay on the ground, his chest barely rising and falling, eyes filled with fear.

No one said a word. Gramps arrived last and broke through the circle, surveying the gruesome scene.

Ron had shot Papa at close range, puncturing his lungs. It was enough to drop him, but not enough to kill him. And Old Papa, in all his beauty, tucked his gentle face down as if to hide from us. Blood seeped from his chest and his enormous body quivered.

Gramps's nostrils flared as he turned to Ron. "What did you do?"

Indignant but aware that he had crossed an invisible line, Ron stepped forward in his own defense.

"He walked right out in the open. I mean, there were kids here, for Christ's sake!"

Gramps's icy stare didn't falter and his voice was equally frigid as he asked again. "What did you do?"

"I was in the lodge getting a drink, and I heard noises out here, so I looked out and saw him." The air around the circle was heavy and dark and Ron's voice rose with anxiety. "I ran out to the garage and got the gun out of the cabinet."

The circle remained silent.

"When I came back, he was still here. So, I shot."

The silence dissolved his pious conviction.

"I mean, what was I supposed to do? He was out in the middle of the yard. What if he attacked one of the kids?"

Gramps's voice boomed, and we jumped. "He was after the pig drippings!"

In one forceful sweep, Gramps grabbed the shotgun away from Ron, who stumbled. Despite the silence, electricity surrounded us. I held my breath in anticipation.

Gramps's eyes bore into Ron as he spoke to the rest of us. "Take the children away."

Ron took a step forward. "What would you have—"

"Go!" Gramps pointed to Ron's cabin.

Ron hesitated a moment, looked at the ground, his teeth gnashing in humiliation, then turned on his heels and stomped off. The children were gathered and ushered away, followed by the rest of the family.

The last in line, Dannie and I started toward the beach, but then I paused and turned back. Barely breathing, I peered around the building's corner.

Alone in the yard, Gramps stood over Old Papa and stared down at the enormous, elderly body. Slowly, Gramps's head dropped forward, shaking sadly, his shoulders hunched forward as he sighed. With measured movements so as not to scare the animal further, Gramps kneeled in front of Old Papa. The bear's moist eyes were frightened, exhausted, their light slowly dying. One paw moved limply, as if he could still make a run for it.

Gramps tenderly laid his hand on Old Papa's neck and stroked him gently, then turned his pained face to the sky and shook his head one last time. With his hand still resting on the thick fur, Gramps whispered.

"I'm sorry, my old friend."

Then Gramps stood. I turned my face away as the gunshot rang out.

As if moving through fog, I made my way to the beach and stared out on the calm lake, my mind void. There was no comprehending such violence and senselessness. We had lost a family member, a piece of fabric that had been woven into our lives. Old Papa was gone, and a part of me broke with his passing.

Out of the corner of my eye, I saw two figures at the end of the dock. Dad was placing a blanket around my mother's shoulders as she sat cross-legged. He kissed her on top of her head as she took his hand. They stared silently until Mom gently waved him off. Dad walked away, his shoulders slightly bent and his head hanging low, his posture reflecting how we all felt.

My eyes stayed on Mom as I shuffled to her side and slid down next to her. She didn't acknowledge my presence, just continued to stare toward the setting sun. My head found its way to her shoulder, and we sat until I couldn't stand it any longer.

"I'm sorry," I whispered.

Mother nodded her head twice. "I can't believe Ron did that."

"No. I mean, I'm sorry for shouting at you."

That broke her trance as she leaned her head to look at me. Still, she said nothing. A sob caught in my throat, and I apologized again. "I don't know why I was acting like such a jerk. I'm sorry." I looked up at her face to see her cheeks were wet.

"Oh, my baby boy." She wrapped her arms around me. The dam broke and tears flowed from the depths of my heart. I tried to speak with only a hiccup erupting.

I heard Mom swallow hard. "This wasn't supposed to happen, you know. Not yet anyway. And there is no wrong or right way for dealing with death, especially when it comes before you expect it."

And there it was. Death on our doorstep. She didn't say it outright, but my mother wasn't just talking about how I was dealing with death. She was also speaking for herself.

"I wanted to go back to teaching. After you and your brothers left for college. And I wanted to go to Italy. I've never been. I was going to…"

I again thought of Mom as her own person. How many things in her life was she now regretting? Things she had never tried. Or worse, things she had done for far too long. She was caregiver, housekeeper, food-prepper, supporter. She had sacrificed so much time for me and for my brothers. Sacrificed for my father. Sacrificed her own dreams and wishes without a word of complaint. And now it was too late.

I gulped back another wave of tears. "I don't know what I'm going to do. What are any of us going to do…after?"

My mother looked up at the sky and blinked hard. "God knows I've been asking that same question on a loop. I won't lie to you, Adam. I think it's going to be difficult." She paused. "It's already difficult."

A loon ascended from underwater and cried.

There was no return call.

I felt Mom's arms grow heavy around me, the weight of her worry physically taking hold. Quietly, she began to recite a poem I had heard a thousand times in our house, the meaning suddenly strangling my heart: *Do Not Stand at My Grave and Weep.*

Into the empty space before us, I whispered, "Mary Elizabeth Frye."

Mom smiled and feigned shock. "So you *have* been listening to us!" I couldn't help but give a small laugh as the animosity I feared she had for me since our fight dissolved.

"You could have picked a less predictable poem, you know."

Mom laughed. "Okay, smartie. You pick one."

I closed my eyes and Wordsworth's *Ode* poured out.

Her smile faded. "You win."

The dark evening had enveloped us, the only light coming from the lodge far behind. My fingers wrapped around my mother's T-shirt and held tight.

"I don't want you to die."

Her chest heaved once. "I don't want to, either."

We sat in silence until she looked at the sky again and smiled softly. "Do you see the North Star?"

"Yes."

"When the time comes—when you're feeling sad, or lost, or lonely—I want you to find the North Star and remember this night. Remember that I told you I love you and I'm always with you. Even when it feels like I'm not."

IT WAS EERILY still the next morning at the beach. The family gathered on lawn chairs and patio furniture pulled from the front porch. They sipped coffee and hot tea, catatonic, staring out over the glassy lake. In front of me sat Mom, Patty, and Tammy, shoulder to shoulder as they leaned into each other. Dad sat alone, as did Richard, brows furrowed in thought. The Feathers huddled on a blanket thrown on the beach's sand, finding security in one another. Even Gramps and Grannie sat side by side as Grannie tenderly held his great, leathered hand.

The only adult absent was Ron.

I sat in a chair next to Dannie, who handed me her orange juice and rested her head on my shoulder. I took a sip as sadness sank its claws deeper into everyone's hearts.

Out of the corner of my eye I saw thunderclouds moving in. We watched in silence as the clouds rolled and rumbled, growing more threatening as they drew near. Dannie took my hand and we joined in the silent sorrow of our makeshift funeral.

Then, one soft droplet after another, the warm rain fell.

No one moved as Mother Nature wept.

Chapter 23

The rain did not break the heat, but intensified the
humidity, so we decided to blow off the steam by
finishing another round of the volleyball tournament.
Dannie and I attempted to spike the ball directly into each
other, which resulted in my receiving a punch in the arm.

"Goddamn it's hot," Angie bellowed. "Paul, crack me a
beer!"

"You got it, Captain." Springing up, Paul retrieved the
cooler and passed around the cold cans, including one for
Dannie. He pushed play on the boombox, cranking the
volume as loud as it would go. Phil Collins overtook the air
and the mood soon changed, as if the morning had never
happened. The cousins' jovial banter and spirited manner
returned. We positioned ourselves, ready to serve the ball
and spirited verbal jabs when Terry came around the corner.

He shook his head. "Count Tabitha out."

"Too hung over?" Eric snorted.

"Nope. Although I'm sure she is. She got into the vodka
lemonade last night and one thing led to another. She called
me a few creative names, packed up her bags, and stumbled
out the door."

My mind immediately raced to the image of her and Ron,
their bodies entangled right outside of the girls' bunk with
me and Dannie listening. *Good riddance.*

The cousins looked at each other and began to snicker.
Terry nodded in agreement. "Yeah, and she took my car.

Paul, I'm going to have to hitch a ride home with you next week."

Paul groaned. "Okay, but I'm in charge of the snack choices."

"Why?"

"Last time we took a road trip together, you downed two chili dogs with extra onion. Then an hour later you topped it off with a bag of Funyuns. I had to have my car fumigated."

"So, not the type of gas you were hoping he'd pitch in for?" Angie laughed.

"Man, the dude was funky."

Laughter rose again.

"What do we do for a player?" I asked.

"I guess we need to ask L.A. Woman," Angie suggested with a sneer as Paul did his best Jim Morrison impression.

"L.A. Woman?" Dannie asked.

"Yeah, that babysitter chick." Eric chuckled. "She was telling us how she's going to pack up and move to L.A. as soon as she leaves here."

I tensed.

"That girl is cuckoo for Cocoa Puffs, if you ask me." Angie circled her finger around her ear. I felt my face redden and turned away to find Dannie staring, a peculiar look on her face.

"Who cares as long as she can serve the ball? Does anyone know where she is?"

It occurred to me that she'd been on my mind nonstop, but I hadn't actually seen much of Amy the last couple of days.

Everyone agreed to spread out and find her. Paul and Katie went to the lodge, Dannie and I to the boys' and girls' cabins, Terry to the beach, and Eric and Angie to the farthest cabins.

Dannie and I walked in silence. A new heaviness had fallen over her. Finally, she muttered, "I don't want her hanging with us. She's a babysitter. Not family. Not a friend. Not a"—she paused for a split second, but long enough to let me know she knew—"not a girlfriend."

I didn't answer.

We checked the girls' cabin, which was empty, then went to the boys' bunk, only to find Tommy and Mikey with a large pad of paper and crayons spread everywhere.

"What are you guys doing?" Dannie asked as she kneeled by Tommy.

"Drawing superheroes. This one is me!" He held up a colorful and enthusiastically scribbled sheet.

"Where's Amy?"

Tommy shrugged. "I don't know. She told us to draw. Said she'd be back later."

Dannie and I exchanged looks and got up to leave when shouting erupted outside. We walked out of the cabin and heard it again, an angry and loud commotion coming from the upper cabins. "You two stay here," Dannie said over her shoulder as we made our way toward the ruckus.

When we reached the top and understanding set in, Dannie took a step back.

Eric and Angie were squared off against Ron and Amy. Amy stood slightly behind Ron, and both were disheveled.

"How can you do this? How can you do this *here*?" Eric shouted at Ron.

"I don't know what you're talking about."

Angie's face was red with rage. "Oh please! I saw you through the window!"

"You always go around looking in windows?"

"You are a pervert," Eric said. "She's a baby."

Amy stiffened.

The yelling attracted the attention of people down at the lodge. As they rushed up the hill, I took Dannie's hand and moved her to the side, away from the arriving adults. The rest of the Feathers came, followed by Tammy, Mom, and Patty, with Richard and Dad close behind. Farther down, I could see Grannie and Gramps slowly winding up the path, their faces intense.

After a quick once-over, hovering for a moment on Ron and Amy, Tammy asked, "What's going on here?"

Angie didn't give Ron or Amy a chance to speak. "I was passing by the cabin when I glanced over and saw Ron and Amy in the bedroom. Together."

No one moved or said a word. Ron and Patty stared at each other, a million shouts and accusations, arguments and verbal assaults conveyed through their eyes. Amy glanced at the surrounding mob and sank farther behind Ron.

"What are you thinking?" Richard asked, astonished.

"Man, it's none of your business what I do with my life."

"She's a child."

"She's eighteen."

"She's sixteen!" Mark barked.

Ron blanched and shot daggers at Amy.

Richard jumped back in. "Even if she *was* legal, this is your family. Your wife and daughter. Right here. Don't you care if you humiliate and betray them? Right under their noses?"

"We're in love," Amy blurted as she appeared from behind Ron.

I closed my eyes to shut out the words.

Angie rolled her eyes with disgust. "Oh, shut up, babysitter. You don't even count in this whole mess, you piece of shit. You are *nothing*. Got it?"

Amy sulked and slid behind Ron again.

Mom stepped forward just as Grannie and Gramps arrived. Her force and power surprised us as the strong woman Dad had hinted at burst forth.

"Ron, we have all stood by and watched while you slowly brought my wonderful cousin down with you. You have been suffocating her, killing her bit by bit with your arrogance, which, by the way, is completely unfounded. You are the biggest buffoon I have ever met. You are a coward. You are a disgusting pig. You are dirty, you are lazy, and you are a drunk. But despite all of that, we stood by without a word because Patty was adamant about making her marriage last. Now? No. I will stay silent no longer. None of us will. This family"—she gestured to everyone around her—"we are a pride of lions. We defend each other, we fight for each other, and we protect each other. You are nothing but a scavenger and you have no place among us. You have destroyed your marriage and your family, and I will not allow you to destroy anything else. You are a toxin that I will no longer allow to poison us. You will not hurt

Patty anymore. You will not hurt Dannie anymore. And you will certainly never step foot in this camp or any of our homes again. You are unwelcome. I suggest you pack your bags and leave immediately." She turned to Amy. "You too."

We stood, mouths agape, awed by my mother.

"Here, here," Angie snorted.

"Time to take the trash out," Eric spit.

Pumped with adrenaline, Ron turned on Eric. "What did you say?"

"I said the trash—that's you—is finally being taken out."

Ron stepped forward and socked Eric square on his broken nose. Eric fell to the ground as blood poured down his face.

"You motherfucker!" Eric gurgled through the blood.

Paul jumped over a writhing Eric and threw a left hook that caught Ron in the jaw. He followed up with another left and Ron, his head bobbing and dizzy, stumbled backwards.

Gramps stepped forward and Paul—his fist in the air, ready for another blow—retreated in deference to the family patriarch. Ron held his jaw and looked around with contempt. Gramps waited until Ron fully focused his eyes, then held his gaze.

"You heard my daughter," he growled. "Leave."

Ron stared at Gramps for a moment, then turned, went inside the cabin, and grabbed a set of car keys.

Gramps shook his head. "The car is Patty's. You can walk."

Ron started to protest, "We're miles from anywhere." He looked around at the men, all of them ready to pounce, and dropped his complaint. With a grunt, he started down the blue stone path leading to the driveway.

Amy looked around in confusion. "How am I getting home?"

Gramps didn't flinch. "You walk, too."

Her eyes darted from person to person as she searched for a sympathetic face.

She found none.

WHEN THE CROWD dissolved and Dannie had disappeared, I went to Amy's cabin. She was crying, throwing her clothes into a duffle bag. I stayed just outside of the screen door.

"Why did you do it?"

Amy looked up, surprised. She barely regarded me as she stuffed a shirt in her bag. "Do what?"

"Why did you spend time with me? How come we had…" My embarrassment kept me from finishing.

She stopped packing and, for a moment, I saw her crack. Her eyes flickered. "I just…I don't know. You were really nice to me. The whole family was. I guess it just felt good. Like I was a part of it all."

"And why him?"

She sighed and continued to throw in shampoo and various items. "I told you already."

"What?"

"Sex is power."

I almost laughed. "You think Ron is powerful?"

She turned to me with a fierceness I didn't expect. "I was going to move out to L.A. and be on his golf show. Like, the host. I was going to be on TV and be famous. It's his show and he chose me, so yeah, I think he's powerful."

I could only shake my head. I finally heard it. What everyone else already had. What my hormonal brain had blocked out. She was like Ron. She was poison. And for all her show of maturity and knowledge, behind her beauty and sexuality, at her core Amy was a scared and lonely teenage girl who hurt others to make herself feel better. She was lost. I wasn't. But accepting the truth and being at peace with that truth were two very different things. There was no peace. No grace. Only anger and betrayal. I wanted to punch her square in the mouth. Hard. I wanted to call her names, shame her violently, make her feel the pain she caused Dannie and me.

Instead, I turned and walked toward the lodge. Toward my family.

As I rounded a corner, I caught the tail ends—literally — of naked Tommy and the newly naked Mikey. It was one thing for Mikey to play with Tommy, but quite another to streak through the camp at eight years old. I called out and ran after the two. Mikey looked behind, saw me coming, and sped up. I quickly caught and tackled him while he threw light, harmless punches at my chest and arms.

"Jesus, Mikey. What are you doing?"

"I'm punching you," He said, grunting with all his might.

"No, you idiot. I mean why are you running around naked?"

"Why not? Tommy is."

"Yeah, but Tommy's four. He's like a baby still." I held both of Mikey's wrists in one hand as he wriggled.

"So am I!"

I frowned. "You're not a baby. Quit wiggling around." I shoved him to the side, where he collapsed, then scooted next to him.

He was pouting and his lower lip quivered slightly. "I am a baby. Just like Tommy."

"Oh really? You need a babysitter, too?"

"No. Mom takes care of me."

I looked hard at Mikey. "You want to be a baby? A baby that Mom has to take care of?" He looked at me sideways and dropped his head slightly. "You think if you don't grow up then she has to stick around to take care of you? Is that it?"

Mikey looked at the ground as tears filled his eyes. I sighed and put my arm around him. "I don't want her to go anywhere either. Believe me. I want her to take care of me, too."

Mikey looked up, eyes round, his face stricken with grief. "I don't want her to die."

I pulled him in close and hugged him hard, rocking him as Mom had done with me so many times. We rocked as dragonflies scooped up mosquitos. Starlings and martins swooped and glided. A swallow chased a crow up above the tree line, and a row of ants marched over a pile of leaves. All around us, we watched life continue as I rocked him and rocked him and held him tight.

Chapter 24

"**W**hat is this?" Gramps grunted. He stared at the plate in front of him. Tammy glanced at Mom and grinned. Mark took a deep breath.

"It's our dinner tonight, Gramps."

"I know you cooked dinner tonight. I just don't know what it is."

"It's called fusion. It's a really big trend in the city."

Gramps continued to stare at the small orange-and-green disk on his plate. "But what *is* it?"

Tentatively, Kelly appeared behind Mark as he tried to explain. "Well, we thought we'd take Up North food and prepare it in the style of what we eat in the city. So, this is sweet potato over a basil puree."

Gramps's brows furrowed into a scowl. "Is this my dinner?"

Kelly tried unsuccessfully to hide the frustration in her voice. "It's part of your dinner. There are other courses. We decided to incorporate Black Bear Lake with Chicago. See? *Fusion*. Everything we made was cooked over the fire pit."

Dad gave Mark a sympathetic smile as Richard scooped up his entire portion onto a fork and swallowed, nodding his approval.

Gramps lifted his plate to scrutinize the vegetables. "There better be thirty more *courses* in the kitchen."

Grannie tried to turn his mood around. "Well, it certainly is something new."

Gramps swiveled around to face Kelly. "Is this what they teach you in your Junior League? This is what you get from going out to lunch every day?"

Kelly sucked in her breath.

He turned to Mark, "I'm surprised you haven't starved to death yet."

Grannie leaned in and whispered. "Charles, stop that now."

"What? I work hard all my life so I can have no dinner at the end of the day?"

Kelly was near tears as Grannie pushed her chair out, "I'll go plate up some leftover spaghetti dinner."

Mark ushered Kelly out of the dining room, and we could hear her ranting all the way to the kitchen.

"Dad, that was terrible," Mom said, stifling a laugh. Gramps grunted again but gave a mischievous grin that sent her into a sincere fit of laughter.

After dinner, we snuck into the kitchen to grab our own small bowls of Grannie's spaghetti, quickly consuming it before Kelly could see us.

"You have to admit, that was pretty genius," Angie said while sucking a noodle into her mouth. My brow creased in confusion as I shoveled in a forkful of the spaghetti.

Eric explained. "Fucking gas is out again, but Grannie didn't want Gramps to know."

"Place is falling apart." Paul sighed as he fiddled with the stove controls, hoping to magically bring it to life.

Eric continued. "Smart woman. Too much for the old man to handle in one day." He winked as he bit into one of Genevieve's dry biscuits and pretended to choke.

Angie snorted. "Love Mark taking one for the team. Fire pit *fusion*. Classic!" She nodded at the door as she swallowed one last bite.

The Feathers filled up their arms with beers and headed out to the bonfire. Mom and Tammy grabbed Patty and retired to the bar to talk. Patty's eyes were swollen from crying, and the women descended on her with outstretched arms. I hadn't seen Dannie since the incident earlier in the day. I hadn't looked for her, deciding she probably wanted to be left alone.

The bonfire was ablaze but the sky was clear and black, a million stars winking down at us. The night seemed to beckon us to the beach, to be together, to share our quiet songs and familial love. I sat on a log stump while Paul strummed a guitar and Angie swayed gently as she sang. My thoughts floated to Amy. I knew I didn't love her, but we shared a bonding experience, to say the least. What happened should have had weight, should have meant *something*. But it hadn't. She'd used me. And worse, she told me beforehand that was how she operated.

For the first time since her betrayal, I allowed myself to feel the pain, not just the anger. It left me empty, a hollow pit drained of all the hope. Gone were the excitement and expectation that first experience had brought. Hot tears fill my eyes.

Suddenly the singing, the hugging, my cousins—it all was too much.

I began to walk toward the blue stone path when I saw Dannie sitting alone at the end of the dock. As I approached, I saw beer bottles strewn around the pier as if she had been there for hours.

"Hey." I sat down gingerly, attempting to gauge her mood.

Dannie threw her head backward and shook it, a slight smile on her face. She passed me a half-full bottle of warm beer, then cracked open another and took a long drink.

I tried to pass the bottle back. "No thanks." But she shot me an angry glance, so I pretended to take a small sip.

"It's all over now, you know." She stared out at the lake, her expression somber.

"What is?"

"The whole thing. All this…bullshit…my dad, my mom…this bullshit…" She was stumbling over her words, but her passion and anger were clear.

"That really was bullshit, what happened this morning. I'm sorry." I put my hand on hers. She looked down as if she couldn't figure out what was touching her, then looked back at the lake.

"No, you're not."

I tilted forward, confused. "What do you mean? Of course I'm sorry. It sucked and you didn't deserve that. You haven't deserved any of it."

Her eyes were full of tears when she turned to me. "Why her?"

"I don't know."

"What was so special about her?"

"Jeez, I have no idea. I mean, your dad—"

"Do you love her?"

My body went hot and cold at once. She wasn't just talking about her dad. She was talking about me.

"No. I don't love her."

"Then why did you pick her over me?"

I just looked at her, clueless.

"Why did my dad pick *her*? What was so special about *her*? Why does everyone love *her* and not me?"

"I do love you, Dannie." My heart broke for her, and I wanted desperately to take her pain away, to give her a reason to put her head on my shoulder, for us to be as we had always been. Together.

The depth of Amy's neediness was too much to bear. She had destroyed, in one way or another, a part of everyone she encountered. I didn't try to explain to Dannie what I had finally figured out, how Amy had just been trying to have what we have, that we were only blue stones on her path to a fulfillment that would never come.

Dannie looked at me. A rivulet of tears coursed across her cheeks.

She turned back to the lake swayed slightly. "Do you hear that? That's our song."

I strained but didn't hear anything. "What?"

She stood on unsteady legs. "The loons. Do you hear them?"

Then I heard. One sad cry that broke the silence of the night. Just one, soft and unobtrusive, floating on the lake air. I smiled at her reassuringly. "Yes, now I do."

She gazed down on me fondly, stumbled slightly, then regained balance. "That's what I want to be. A loon." She closed her eyes. "Gliding. Peacefully. And when danger comes—when you just can't stand to be vulnerable anymore—down you go. Weightless in the water, down as deep as you can swim, till the only thing surrounding you is silence. And comforting darkness." She lifted her arms out to her sides, her eyes still closed and smiled. "I want to be a loon." And with that, she dove straight into the lake, disappearing into the black water.

"Dannie!" I yelled, but she didn't resurface. I scanned the water, searching for any sign of where she went. Nothing. I screamed again, then saw a wave of movement from deep below. Without hesitation, I dove in after her. Blind in the lake, I swept my legs and arms wide until I skimmed one of her limbs. I shot out and, with a vice grip, pulled her to the surface, both of us gasping for air. I slowly swam her in until we could touch the lake bottom.

As soon as we had solid sand under our feet, I turned to her. "What the hell! You almost drowned."

Dannie stood motionless against my anger, as if she couldn't hear me, then took a step closer. She put her hands around my neck and held me tighter than she ever had before. "You are the only person in the world who loves me." Suddenly, snapped out of her intoxicated trance, her face twisted up and she let out a loud sob. As fast as she could, she broke through the water, reached the shore, and dashed up the beach, swiping a pack of cigarettes lying next to Angie as she fled toward the girls' cabin.

Reeling, I moved slowly toward shore, my soaked clothes clinging to me, weighing me down even more. I walked past the bonfire and thought of Amy. She had invaded everything that meant anything to me. I pulled out my notebook, the last few pages filled with scribblings about a desperate longing for a girl with long auburn hair. With a heavy heart, I threw the lake-soaked notebook in the fire.

Watching flames lick the edges of soggy paper, I lost myself in thought. My summer dream had come true, but it was far from what I'd imagined. My vision had consisted of laughter, bare skin skimming in a pool, possibly a girlfriend that I would walk hand-in-hand with through the school doors in the fall. The reality had been a meltdown of everything I knew and loved. My family system was failing all around me and, for the first time in my life, I knew they were all that truly mattered. Every part of my being—my interests, my ideals, my ideas of right and wrong—they were also woven into everyone at Black Bear Lake. My deepest secrets, my value of love, my sense of loyalty all came from threads that tied me to my family. My competitive drive, albeit lacking in skill, came from Aunt Tammy. My occasional gruffness from Gramps. My playfulness from Eric. My tenderness from my mother. And Dannie. My Dannie. It was impossible to sense where one of us ended and the other began.

The love I sought had been with me all along.

I paused a moment longer to watch the edges of my notebook begin to curl brown. Dragging my feet up the path to the girls' cabin, I rehearsed several conversations in my head, ways to handle the situation. I would tell Dannie her whole family loved her. That the embarrassment of her father would pass, as would her feeling of hopelessness. I would say that she could come live with my family while her parents worked out all the ugly details, that she wouldn't have to be an outcast at school anymore, that she…

Chapter 25

I sat in the dirt, dazed, completely disoriented and clueless as to what had just happened. I'd been knocked backward off my feet, as if an invisible bully had shoved me full force with both hands. Had a large firecracker gone off? Were Kevin and his cronies messing around in the woods? I searched the sky but saw nothing, not even the moon and stars.

I paused for a moment, then moved fast.

My animal instincts told me to run. I didn't know I was running or where I was running to, but something was wrong. The woods, the pathway, the cabins were all pitch black. Clouds covered the full moon, and I could barely make out the path. I stumbled on newly fallen trees that resembled an overturned box of matches. As I neared the top of the hill, I heard low moaning. I passed the boys' cabin, the windows all blown out, the roof caved in on one side. When I looked toward the girls' cabin, I stopped in my tracks unsure of what I was seeing.

Or, rather, what I was *not* seeing.

The clouds moved and the bright moonlight illuminated the scene.

The cabin was gone.

Pieces of wood were strewn everywhere. Only one wall still stood. The roof was completely missing, and the insulation had fallen gracefully, like pink snowflakes blanketing the surrounding ground. Boards and beams crisscrossed each other, as if someone had knocked over a Lincoln Log home.

Then I found Dannie, trapped, a ceiling beam crushing her pelvic bone. She let out a guttural, animalistic sound.

From behind me I heard shouts and yells as the family tried to figure out what happened. Mothers were calling out for their children, the cousins were calling for each other, and the same phrase kept rising to the surface.

"What was that?"

Blood rushed to my head, my ears started to buzz, and everything moved in slow motion. I ran, tripped, fell, ran again, all the while screaming for help, though I couldn't hear myself. I ran to Eric, who caught me as I tripped again.

"The girls' bunkhouse!" I screamed. "Dannie!"

I couldn't scream loud enough. I still couldn't hear myself. But a rush of relief came over me as I saw recognition in Eric's eyes. He dropped me and ran for the cabin.

Everyone seemed to follow immediately after that and I found myself running with the group, pushing and pulling, trying to make some sense out of utter chaos. I heard voices that sounded far away, asking me what happened and to stop screaming. But I *still* couldn't hear myself and felt as if we were moving through quicksand. My mouth was moving, telling everyone to hurry, not understanding that I had screamed myself hoarse. I fell again and Richard pulled me to my feet, hurrying me along.

We reached the cabin and found Eric as he attempted to pull the beam off Dannie's body. I could see, yet I couldn't. I heard those same far-away voices and knew in my head they were standing right next to me, all screaming in horror and panic.

Richard appeared in front of me, shaking me hard. Finally, as if waking from a dream, I could see him. Hear him. Richard's loud voice remained calm but firm as he directed me. "Go get a ballpoint pen from the lodge. As fast as you can. Run!"

My feet barely touched the ground and I jumped over the few steps connecting the cabin path to the blue stone. I fell on the lodge's landing and slid halfway down, shredding layers of skin from my thighs. I didn't feel a thing. Frantically, I searched through the kitchen drawers. There had to be a pen somewhere. I remembered seeing Grannie writing out recipes. The frenzied forage seemed endless until I finally found one and raced back to Richard.

He unscrewed the pen, dumped out the insides, and inserted the tube into a small slit he had made in Dannie's lower throat. I took Dannie's hand again, unable to look at her wounds. She stared directly into me. I bent down and whispered in her ear.

"I promised I wouldn't leave you. I'm not leaving you."

The men hurried forward to help Eric as he again attempted to free Dannie from the ceiling beam. He counted to three quickly, then they lifted with groans and strained faces. Dannie had stopped moaning and was staring at the sky, blinking absently.

Tammy ran over with a sheet from the boys' cabin, and Richard gave out orders. "We need to move her away from here. And everyone else, too. There might be another explosion." The mothers frantically grabbed children, their own and any others close to them, and whisked them down the hill.

Mom came up next to me and tried to pull me away from Dannie. "Adam, come with me *now!* I don't want you up here." I shrugged her off violently. Dannie's head lolled toward me, and I took her hand again. As gently as they could, the men awkwardly slid Dannie onto the sheet, a makeshift gurney, and lifted the four corners. Dannie's eyes widened and she gasped. "Adam, I'm falling off. Catch me. I'm falling. My legs are sliding off." I moved to lift her leg back onto the sheet.

But there was no leg.

It was as if a magician had performed an optical illusion. Dannie's limb had simply disappeared. Her hipbone was exposed, and long tendrils of flesh and ligaments hung loose.

I froze in horror as Dannie's breathing became more labored.

In the distance, I could hear fire engines arrive, sirens blaring, followed by police cars and an ambulance.

Paul jumped up. "I'll go to the top of the driveway and lead them in."

Behind me, Patty screamed. She had been last to come to the cabin. Tammy and Mom tried to hold her back, but Patty became crazed when she saw her daughter. She broke away and ran toward us, pushing me aside. Patty rocked Dannie in her arms as she wailed. I lost my grip on Dannie's hand, but we stared into each other, a lifetime of friendship, companionship, and love passing between us. I had promised her I wouldn't leave, and I didn't.

I held our gaze after she no longer could.

Chapter 26

The rest of the night and next morning played out like a surreal dream. Although she was pronounced dead at the scene, the ambulance took Dannie away with Patty still clinging to her, overcome with grief. Mom and Tammy followed behind. No one slept and no one spoke. In the light of day, after long discussions, the police and fire department determined that the explosion was the result of a gas buildup in the cabin's upper crawl space. I was interviewed and gave my account, the memory of her heartbroken escape seared in my mind. The police concluded that after leaving me, Dannie came into the cabin and lit one of the cigarettes from the stolen pack. It was just enough of a spark to ignite the gas.

The explosion was nothing like the movies. No big fireball. No burst of flames shooting into the sky. In fact, there were no flames at all. The explosion hadn't ignited anything, but had simply disintegrated everything.

The sound was like the popping of a giant balloon, and the impact hit the windows of nearby cabins, panes cracking and shattering. The force was so great that shingles had flown off the roofs, and beams on the porches buckled and cracked as if Paul Bunyan himself had split them over his knee.

Articles of clothing, books, playing cards, and hairbrushes were strewn out as far as six cabins away. A mattress shot straight in the air by the blast had landed in a large pine. The branches pierced it and held it hovering over us, like a bizarre tree house.

I walked round and round the remains of the cabin and hoped to wake up, hoped that there had been some mistake, hoped the night before hadn't happened at all. As I turned to walk away, I noticed a cassette tape in the brush by the side of the path. It was marked in Dannie's writing. *For Adam—Summer 1983.*

My last summer at Black Bear Lake.

Chapter 27

I stood next to Mom and Dad at the funeral. Mom held my
hand tightly and asked if I was all right every ten
minutes. Patty stood on one side of the casket and Ron on
the other. Grannie sat in a chair next to Patty and silently
cried, while Gramps stood behind her. Our family filled in
the areas behind and wide to each side, creating a semi-
circle around Patty. Once again, the family knitted together.
And as Dannie's casket was lowered into the ground, as
Patty lost her balance and fell from her tightrope, the safety
net caught her.

❧

THAT WINTER, I stood again at a gravesite and held my
father's hand. The rest of the family stood behind Dad, my
brothers, and me.

Our cousins, aunts, and uncles slowly left my mother's
gravesite one by one, silently saying goodbye as they threw
in small handfuls of dirt. Tammy came up quietly and stood
by my side.

"Hey kiddo."

"Hey."

"You need anything?" She looked at me softly, but I had
no softness to return, no giving left in me.

I had nothing.

"That's a dumb question."

"I'm going to help clean out the house so you guys don't
have to."

I stood silent.

"Also, I'll freeze all the food that people brought over. Then you can thaw it out as you need it. There's enough to last you a couple years," she said with a smile, trying to be light.

I ignored her.

Tammy paused. "Listen, I know how hard—"

"Leave me alone." I was shocked by the force with which the words flew out and was fully ready for Tammy to walk away, reprimand me, or even to slap my mouth for such disrespect.

Instead, she pulled me in hard and hugged me. I tried to fight, but she wouldn't let go. She just cradled me and swayed until I calmed.

"I won't leave you alone, Adam. We're family."

GRAMPS HAD BEEN right. The deaths were too much and had taken everything from Grannie. She passed away two years after Mom died. And Gramps, lost without the love of his life, followed soon after. I didn't cry at either of their funerals. My tears had run dry. It didn't matter the time of day or what I was doing, the image of Dannie diving into the water haunted me. I barraged myself with questions every night when I closed my eyes: *I knew she was teetering on the edge, so why didn't I go check on her sooner? Why had I wasted time burning that damn notebook instead of immediately following her up to the cabin? Why hadn't I told my mother she was drinking away her pain every day that summer? Why hadn't I told Patty she was being bullied at school?*

The answer to every question ended with a scenario that would have saved her. If I'd have just done something, *anything*, Dannie would still be alive. But I'd done nothing. I wasn't a good friend. I wasn't a good cousin. I was selfish, my whole summer centering solely on Amy. I ignored the most important thing in the world to me, and it cost a life. Dannie's life. I swore to myself I would never make the same mistake again. Never would I allow someone so close to my heart. Never would I be responsible for another's soul and well-being. I couldn't be trusted to protect another. I was lethal.

It wasn't until several years later that Patty, who had taken over Gramps's fight when he passed, was awarded compensation for the explosion. She endured over and over the horrific story of Dannie's death. Every hearing reopened the wound in her heart, every document she read and signed. When the legal nightmare was finally over and the gas company was found negligent, Patty received a windfall settlement.

No one said a word, but we all knew the truth: The money meant nothing. It would never repair a disastrous marriage, would never bring my mother back home, would never bring my grandparents back to their family. Dannie was gone and would remain gone. Patty spent little, becoming more reclusive as the years went by.

The full bank account was just an angry reminder of all we'd lost.

Chapter 28

MAY 2008

The setting sun sparkled on the chilled lake as I sat on the dock, my bare feet dangling in the water as it had decades before. I'd spent the day wandering the land and pathways I'd known my whole life, this time seeing it through new eyes. The lodge was no longer the mammoth building of my youth. The cabins were worn, roofs caving in from neglect. The beach had eroded, and the bonfire pit had been overtaken with weeds.

The magic was gone.

As I looked back, the time before Dannie's death and the time after seemed like night and day. We weren't the same, any of us. A crack had begun to deteriorate and rust in all of us.

During the years that followed the quick procession of tragedies, I did my job as oldest brother. I went through the motions and helped Dad raise our family. Helped us survive. The days passed without event, months melting into years, years melting into a life lived mechanically.

Kevin graduated from high school and took over Gramps's business, quickly doubling its size. He matured from a failing pothead into a local business sensation almost overnight.

Mikey had turned to Richard as a role model and graduated from high school, then medical school, with honors.

During it all, Dad remained quiet and steadfast. His orderliness and disciplined rituals carried him through the day-to-day, but he lost the glimmer I had once seen in him. He was no longer a hero to me. No one was.

I built a protective wall around myself, abandoning everything that had once made up my world. I left behind my words, my poetry, my romanticism. I left behind any childhood innocence. I left behind the feelings of safety and warmth. I left behind the hopes and dreams I once held and the peace that had at one time been woven so deeply into my soul.

I chose a faraway college, then moved far from that place, then moved far again as soon as relationships and friendships began to take root. Then, finally, I settled back in Chicago with Julie.

But even with a home and a job and a wife, nothing felt permanent in my heart. I had moved away from myself after that last summer at Black Bear Lake and had never moved back.

Standing in front of the lake, the memories crushed down on me, and the tears came. Tears that I'd spent half my life holding back. I dipped my finger into the water and felt the connection. Dannie was still here. My mother was still here. Gramps and Grannie, too. They had never left. I had just pushed them away.

I had spent all my energy fighting the memories and the love I thought had been ripped away. But it was all still there, just below the surface. Remembering that summer felt like digging out gravel embedded in an ancient wound. Excruciating but necessary to speed along the healing process.

I desperately wanted to feel the warmth of my family, the security of their net. I wanted to experience laughter and comfort. I wanted to feel vulnerable and know that I was safe. I wanted Julie to lean into me the way Mom had with Dad. I wanted Julie to know that I had chosen her the way Dad had chosen Mom. I remembered Dad wishing he had not tried to control his world so much. Without knowing it, I had followed in my father's footsteps.

But unlike my father, I still had time.

A future waited for me, if only I would embrace my fear of loss. I wanted a life of lightness and dreams. And I wanted to share that life with Julie.

Dr. Marchand was right. I had taken the first step. And it was scary. I didn't know what the next step would be, but I had finally been dislodged. I filled my lungs with air heavy with pine trees, lake water, and youth. It smelled of a different lifetime, one I greatly missed. For the first time since I was fourteen, I didn't feel lost. I wasn't solid or sure, but I felt the seedling of hope.

The stars had begun to pop in the sky, the North Star glittering brightest. Beckoning me.

I reached into my coat, dug out my cell phone, and dialed with shaky hands.

"Hello?"

I smiled through tears as I spoke into the phone. "I'm here, Julie. I'm looking out at the lake. I'd forgotten how beautiful it was. How beautiful it *is*."

"Adam." Her voice was filled with empathy, a softness I hadn't expected, and a fresh wave of tears came over me. She spoke tentatively, as if trying to avoid startling a wild animal. "Are you ok?"

"I am. At least, I think I'm going to be. And I was thinking—" I paused, looking out at the still lake, only a solitary loon breaking the glassy surface.

"If it's a girl, can we name her Dannie?"

Acknowledgments

There are no words that exist to embody the immense gratitude I have for the opportunity to bring *Black Bear Lake* out of the shadows and into the world.

I want to thank the incredibly supportive and collaborative team at Blue Handle Publishing for giving me space to grow this project, and for believing from the beginning that the book mattered. Thank you for allowing me to stand beside you at the helm, steering this ship to a shore we all envisioned together.

A heartfelt thank you to Stephanie, Shari, and Megan, who read, who critiqued, who edited while asking nothing in return. I can never repay your emotional generosity.

To the family who actually lived through this horrific ordeal in your once-cabin on our lake. My heart will always be with you.

To Mom and Dad for making sure books mattered in our lives. You taught me that literature and knowledge are as vital as air and water. None of my writing would exist without your support and encouragement. I owe it all to you.

To Jimmy, the yin to my yang, the puzzle piece that fits perfectly with mine: Thank you for being my biggest champion and making me believe I can conquer this crazy, enormous world.

To my children, every word is for you.

LESLIE LIAUTAUD

For more great titles from Blue Handle Publishing
authors, visit BHPubs.com.

Or you can follow us on social media
Twitter: *@BHPUBS*
Instagram: *@BlueHandleBooks*

Our Founder Charles D'Amico
@Charles3Hats
on all platforms

<u>Other Authors on Instagram</u>

Leslie Liautaud
@author.leslie.liautaud

Jordan Reed
@author.jordan.reed

Andrew J Brandt
@WriterBrandt

Ray Franze
@TheHeightsNovel